Thunderbird Studios Presents

DECADES OF SAN CICARO

Edited by James Fadeley and Ali Habashi

A Thunderbird Studios Publication

Decades of San Cicaro Copyright © 2022 Thunderbird Studios Limited Liability Company. All stories contained within this book are the property of the respective authors. All rights reserved.

Cover Image and design by Manuel Mesones (https://herearedragons.uk)
Book design by James Fadeley (https://jamesfadeley.com)
ISBN 13: 978-1-946289-06-3
ISBN 10: 1-946289-06-X

No part of this publication may be reproduced; stored in a retrieval system, or transmitted in any form or by any means, electronic, mechanical, photocopying or otherwise, without the prior permission of the publishers.

These are works of fiction. All the characters and events portrayed in this book are fictional and any resemblance to incidents and real people, living or dead, is purely coincidental.

Follow Thunderbird Studios at their website or on social media at:

https://www.tbirdstudios.com
Twitter: @tbirdstudios
Facebook: www.facebook.com/ThunderbirdStudiosLLC

Table of Contents

Intern Work	9
Echoes in the Bath House	13
Los Vigilantes Oscuros	28
Slivers	30
A Break	50
Ascension of the USS Fairweather	52
Headline Space for Mysteries	67
Garibaldi Pearls	69
Lunch Break	88
Moonshot	94
Gaps in History	112
Animal Control	114
Between Professionals	136
The Last Obituary for the Old Man	139
Regrets	152
Gold in the West	154
Witness	157
About the Authors	160

Intern Work

"I thought I was finished with this crap," Olivia muttered under her breath as she pulled open the door to the San Cicaro Public Library. The air was stale with old books, and just a faint whiff of mildew that the custodians could never seem to find. Carts of returned titles waited by the glass walls, which became a brick facade the further along she went. Olivia had been faintly disappointed the first time she visited the place—this was the library of San Cicaro itself, self-proclaimed "Strangest City in America." She'd pictured spiral staircases, haunted paintings and all that wizardly pomp. Yet like a lot of stories she covered, the truth tended to be slightly more mundane.

It was early in the morning, so the library was vacant. Just a few dead-eyed students from College University of San Cicaro trying desperately to finish their work before the finals. Olivia was not envious of their situation. At least now she was earning money, instead of spending it to suffer the same stress. Although she wished she merited more respect than she was getting.

Or at least a lighter laptop, she thought, adjusting her bag strap. *This is intern work.*

The only person who didn't seem terribly stressed was the librarian. Olivia slowed, realizing it was a new face and one about her age.

"Excuse me."

He looked up. Taking in all of his features, Olivia realized he was rather cute. Thin, and maybe a little gangly, with clear skin and dark features. He smiled, his voice an even baritone. "Can I help you?"

"My name is Observer, and I'm here for the Olivia."

He stared at her blankly, and she realized her mistake. "Sorry, I haven't had any coffee yet."

He laughed, covering his face to keep the sound from ringing out. Olivia felt her cheeks flush.

"My name is Olivia Murphy, and I'm here for the *San Cicaro Observer*."

"Sure, hang on." The cute librarian flipped some papers on his desk. "Huh. Special permission to use our archives?"

"Ayup."

The desk drawer *thunked* as he opened it, fetching a few keys. Olivia's eyes went up as he stood a solid foot over her. *Tall. Check.*

"So can I ask a question?" he proposed as he led her over the aging carpets towards the elevator.

"Sure."

"Why does the *San Cicaro Observer* need access to our archives? Don't you guys have your own back catalog?"

"We did, but the warehouse storing them caught on fire in the late nineties. Some of our stuff was backed up on disk, but not the really old editions."

"And online archives are worth a few bucks a month?"

"He can be taught!"

He grinned, but put his finger to his lips.

They stopped before an old elevator. Olivia realized she had to walk back on some of her earlier thoughts. Apparently there *were* some spookier things about the library. The librarian inserted a key and pulled the shutters aside with an eerie creak. "After you."

"Um…"

He grinned, and stepped into the car first. It shook only slightly. "Inspected three months ago. It's old, but works fine."

Her anxiety eased, and Olivia stepped inside. "What? No lever?"

He shrugged and pushed the button for the basement level. It shuddered only slightly as they descended. In a few moments, he drew open the cage, and the two stepped out into the archive proper. It was pitch black, until he found the switch.

This was a vision of a corporate underworld. A large, windowless expanse greeted them with beige walls, bland doors, buzzing strip lights and fissured ceiling tiles. Not something you'd see on a brochure, that's for sure.

The only difference between the nondescript doors were the slider sides, portals to magical places like the "utility room" or "storage."

"You sure know how to take a girl out for a night on the town," Olivia said flatly.

"Well, maybe next time, I'll even take you to dinner," he said with a mischievous grin.

"Why? Is there a vending machine in the utility room?"

Point for me, she thought as he burst into laughter. He led her to several old cabinets and pulled one out.

"These contain almost everything from the *San Cicaro Observer* since its founding. Some are missing because of age or theft, but most of them should be available. Do you need the microfiche reader?"

"I brought a portable one," Olivia said, patting her case. "But I could use some table space, a chair and an electrical outlet."

He pointed to a round table in the corner, near a small, high window. Old, plastic chairs with metal legs were gathered around it, reminding Olivia of middle school. As she set her bag down, he pointed at an old corded phone on the wall.

"If you need anything, dial 1 then 9 to reach the front desk. The elevator down here is unlocked, so you can get out. But you'll need to ask me to go down again."

"I appreciate that," Olivia said. "So who do I ask for on the phone?"

"Keanu."

"Like the actor?"

He sighed, eyes half closed. "Mom named me after him."

"Huh. Well thanks… *Mister Reeves!*" She grinned.

"Don't. Just, don't," he replied, but with a knowing smile of his own.

He headed back to the elevator. She took that opportunity to study his butt through his jeans. *Eh, needs some juice in that caboose.*

Having learned her lesson from her first interview a year ago, she made sure to plug in her laptop and the portable microfilm reader. As the machines warmed up, she took a look at the daunting, printed list of articles she needed to seek and copy.

"There's no way I'm finishing this today," she said to herself. There were plenty of editions to find, work left over by the summer interns who had gone back to school. Olivia suspected those were the missing newspapers Keanu mentioned, but she had to check just in case.

After glancing at the list, Olivia began sifting through the archives, the metal drawers *thunking* loudly as she opened them. The microfilm plates stopped at 1938. This gave Olivia pause, then she remembered Melissa mentioning that the newspaper was called *The Cicaro Tribune* back then. No wonder the idiot interns skipped all of the early 30's.

Returning to her desk with a few boxes, she set them down and flipped open the reader. With care, she withdrew a plate with a grid of boxes, and was relieved when she saw no signs of damage. Setting a reel from 1933 editions on the reader's tray, she closed the top, then clicked an application on her laptop.

It was tempting to start the programming script the web editor had given her, but it was a good call to manually align the first page of the newspaper. If the first was off, all of them would be, and there was no way she wanted to be here longer than she had to be.

Until she saw the first headline appear on the screen. She had no idea there was once a bath house in San Cicaro.

Or how it had perished.

Echoes in the Bath House
Adrianna Valencia

A young woman wearing a crimson sweater steps in front of me as I approach the plaque on the blustery cliffside. She has the tiniest cinched waist, which suddenly flares out to the most glorious full tartan skirt. As she steps forward it billows in the salt-spray wind, but she tames it quickly with a stern hand. I look down at my own green beaded dress, glorious in its day. My, how the times have changed. It had once been my favorite, but now it just makes me feel my age… whatever that is. You hit a certain point one day and you just stop counting.

The sky today reflects the concrete ruins that lay skeletal around me. Once vibrant, now gray and flat and sad. I step around the girl in the full skirt to read the sign in front of us. Not that I need to, but I still like to be reminded of when these ruins were not ruins at all. Not an attraction, not a monument to tragedy or a National Recreational Area, but a dream come to life built of steel and sea glass. And perhaps a nightmare or two for those who remember it.

"The Sutton Bath House was built in 1900 by millionaire philanthropist Halston 'Hal' Sutton. Sitting proudly on the cliffs of San Cicaro, it was designed in the Neoclassical grand block style and dubbed "Greatest Seaside Resort" in 1906 by Pacific Lifestyle Magazine. With its grand glass chamber hosting seven temperature-controlled ocean water pools and stunning full views of the Pacific, it was not hard to imagine why."

Beneath a faded illustration of the grand Bath House exterior, a caption read: *"Stay and Play at the Sutton Bath House! circa 1908."*

A grainy browned photograph next to it showed men in swim caps and bathing costumes to their knees. They were lined up in front of one of the massive pools. *"A summer paradise!"*

And it was for many years. It was my father's greatest work, and something he could sink his time and energy into after my mother's sudden passing. He would carry me around the build site as a little girl, regaling me with his plans for the splendid structure yet to be built. He wore a beautifully tailored suit even on site visits, and I remember dust sprinkling his thickly waxed mustache as we strolled the cliffside construction.

There are no pictures of him on these monument plaques.

A gust of wind takes my breath, closing its fist around my throat for one icy moment. But perhaps it's not the wind. Maybe it's the longing for a grandeur that will never be again. Or the memories of watching my father die. Or maybe… it's the creatures who brought this summer palace to its ruin.

I can't feel Them yet, but I know They'll appear in time. They always do on days when I return.

The first time I saw Them I was at my father's deathbed.

We lived in the largest apartment suite at the very top of the Baths. His bedroom window-walls provided panoramic views of the ocean to the west and the mountains to the northeast. When I was a child we would sit on the small couch at the foot of his bed, watching the orange and pink Pacific sunsets set the mountainside ablaze as the gramophone played in the corner. And in those last terrible moments of his life we were surrounded by just such a sunset, although the gramophone sat silent in deference to my screams.

I'd been in the hall on my way to call him for dinner when I heard the gunshot. When I'd found him wounded on his bed, there was no sign of a gunman. Only his pained moans and the fiery mountains and the figures gathering dark in the craggy bluffs. I thought my eyes deceived me, too shocked at my father's perilous state to register what I'd glimpsed briefly in the distance. But as I called for help and went to his side, They commanded my attention.

They seemed only to be the inky silhouettes of vagrants stopping to take in the sunset on the distant trail. But seven or eight of Them steadily took shape from nothing and nowhere, like thick Monterey fog seeping into a human mold.

Their void-like darkness reflected nothing, even in the fiery light of the sunset. But Their eyes… they cut through everything. I was blinded by those piercing spotlights trained in my direction. I still remember the horror from knowing that somehow, They knew I had seen Them—that I had watched Them materialize. And They were watching me back.

Through his moans and delirium, my father knew too.

"I failed you, my little love…"

He rasped at me, trying to wrench free of my grip to hold my hands. I couldn't take my eyes off the mountains and the figures staring unflinchingly back. "Do not forget… every year, promise me… *do not forget.*"

I pressed down on his chest trying to slow the bleeding, too dumbstruck with fear and shock to decipher his words in those final moments. Yet I remember the moment his eyes gripped mine in a frenzy of urgency and fear.

When I looked up again, the shadowy figures were closer, at the foothills now. Terror, sharp and electrified, brought my bloody hand to my face. They grew impossibly darker as the sun grew weaker and the mountains redder. And Their spotlight eyes grew brighter.

"The letter in my desk…" he pointed then to his roll-top in the corner. "Read and understand… then burn it. Swear to me…"

His body slackened weakly against the looming wooden headboard. His gaze softened hazily.

"Father, I don't—please don't go…"

As I let go of his chest in a frenzy of panic, the bullet wound erupted in blood. In that moment I knew he was nearly gone, and I clutched him to me. The bed was warm and wet, and the rusty odor of gore and despair overwhelmed me.

Through my tears and screams, I squinted out across the mountainside again. The figures had somehow reached the beach, standing in a line from shore to deeper water, facing me. They were solid and motionless like piers on the boardwalk, their searchlight eyes piercing the growing dusk, bright and unflinching. They were waiting for something.

I heard hurried footsteps—too human to be shadows—making their way through the halls. They may have been coming to help, or they may have been fleeing the scene. It doesn't matter anymore. Although my father's killer was never arrested, his murderers were just outside watching from the sea.

My father's last breaths rattled wetly under my embrace as the Watchers dissolved into the fine spray of the Pacific.

The last time I saw Them, I was too late.

It was 1933, and the Sutton Bath House no longer earned the title of Greatest Seaside Resort. When I was a little girl, my father would call it, "the Western pinnacle of Eastern elegance." He would smile and jab at the sky with dramatic flair while I laughed. And truly it was, once.

Most of the draw was the glamor of the Baths. Everyone from Duke Ellington to Anna May Wong to Calvin Coolidge retreated here for a short time, many on their way to visit Hearst at his castle. The Sutton Bath House was both a playground for the wealthy and elite and a seaside escape for folks of other walks of life. Despite the occasional… unusual disappearances surrounding the Baths, we'd helped put San Cicaro on the map. One or two annual disappearances loosely tied to our establishment were easy to overlook. These people had no idea of the real horrors that lay dormant in the mountains just across the highway.

But my father's death seemed to seep into the very foundations of the Bath House. The Great Crash was not far behind his passing, bringing with it financial ruin and the slow decline of this once great summertime destination. Most would say it was the Crash that brought the Baths into disrepair.

If only that were true.

"Good evening, madam," the stocky maître d' greeted me stiffly at the dining room door, taking my evening wrap from my shoulders. "The usual table?"

"If you don't mind, Guillermo."

We wound our way through the grand dining hall toward the floor-to-ceiling wall of glass, tables lit with tapered candles and draped in slightly threadbare linens. The Seaglass Room, once bursting with the tinkling of glasses and chatter and opulence, now lay mostly barren. Only a few early diners sipped at their first soup course.

Guillermo sat me at my table for one, which overlooked the magnificent Bath House pool chamber below. There were seven Olympic sized pools in all, the strong summer sun dazzling through the fifty-foot reinforced glass walls that overlooked the ocean. Bathers swam and played in each temperature-controlled ocean water pool, diving from floating platforms trapezes, springboards or from catwalks scaffolding the second level. A grand iron staircase sloped gracefully from the second level of the opposite wall. As visitors descended into the humid glass house of the pool chamber, it gave them a brief taste of glamor and grandeur.

It struck me that this was my father's real legacy. Joy and freedom—the ability to lose yourself in enjoyment and leisure for one afternoon, regardless of your family life or your income or your social status. It was because of this living and breathing dream that I was bound to maintain this place, whatever the cost. But the cost was much more than our fortune alone could fulfill.

Despite the late August warmth, dread spread cold and languid through me. This day is never a good day. The sun was sinking towards the horizon. I needed to find a suitable offering quickly. I estimated that I had a few hours left, not much time to find what I needed and drive up to the mountain pass.

Guillermo set an iced tea to my right. What I wouldn't give for a dry martini at The Golden Pearl.

"Is there anything more I can do for you, madam? Perhaps some oysters this evening?"

"Guillermo... do you know what day it is?"

He paused, his gaze hardening as he held mine. Sea lions barked and splashed faintly in the distance. "Yes madam. I do indeed."

"Sit down please, won't you?"

"Of course, madam," he replied stiffly. I distinctly remember him adjusting his black bowtie with professional resolve before pulling out his own chair and sitting down. It was little things like this that made me think of my father

"What day is today, Guillermo?" I questioned, my heartbeat drumming in my ears while I attempted to remain icy.

"It… it is a day of much sadness for the Sutton Bath House, madam," he responded slowly, diplomatically.

"Come now, please don't make me repeat myself, Guillermo. You and I both know it's much more than that."

He shifted uncomfortably now in his tuxedo, glancing into the harsh sun.

"Please madam, I have grandchildren at home. *Nietos*," he uttered automatically, forgetting himself in his discomfort.

I softened slightly.

"And what are your grandchildren's names?"

"Ernest. Ernest and Lucy—*Lucia*," he said quietly, looking down at the white linen tablecloth. "She will be five in September."

"I expect that will be a very special day for you. One that could not be missed," I met his eyes and put my hand on his arm. He wiped the sweat from his forehead, smiling weakly in relief.

"No madam, it would be the greatest sadness of my life."

"Right. Then tell me, Guillermo," I sat up straight again. "What do you know of the Watchers?"

Guillermo froze, his face taking on a faint pallor. His lips parted slightly as he found his words.

"Mi abuela, she would tell me stories… when I was a boy, I watched her lay down offerings of fruit and sweets by the shed after every harvest," he began, visibly filing through his memories. "We would look out onto the fields at dusk, and she would tell me that these gifts pleased the Watchers. As long as They were given an offering, They would watch over the valley. They would bring blessings to our crops and our families."

He paused, clutching his drink tray in a way that reminded me of a child sitting in the headmaster's office.

"But what could this possibly… then the rumors are true?"

"You've been with us for some thirty years now, Guillermo. You never before suspected that they were true?"

He looked at me with terrified apprehension, awaiting the horrors that lay within my forthcoming explanation.

"With Samson's departure last Spring, I'm looking for a new man," I said. "I've been remiss in leaving the… interview process, until now. But it's an unpleasant task. For me more than it was for Samson, though he ultimately chose to leave… a luxury I do not possess."

I took a sip of my iced tea and looked out over the pools. Nautical soft light filtered in, hazy through the thin layer of salt and dust coating the glass. Hollow echoes bounced across the ceiling at random as a few remaining guests splashed in the lonely pools. I needed to focus. Time was ebbing dangerously.

"My point is that there is a reason that both fortune and tragedy have befallen the Baths. There's a reason that my father died such a terrible death. He had failed the Watchers. He had refused to leave an offering because it had become too much."

The maître d' looked confused. "But madam, surely with such a fortune as your father's he could have spared some food at the time—"

"The maintenance and protection of such a large and much-beloved structure has demanded an offering more significant than crops," I interrupted bluntly, softening no blows.

In that moment the Bath House stopped completely. No glasses tinkled, no bathers splashed, no waves were heard crashing in the distance. It seemed as if the entire world had heard my words and condemned me for them. I carried on.

"My father unknowingly built on Watcher land. There were symbols… he hadn't known what they meant until They came to him one night on the beach, peered into his mind and made him see. This place was sacred to Them, and he owed Them a far greater offering to prevent tragedy and destruction from befalling this place.

"So, he paid. First in workers, then in vagrants. And now it's up to me to pay… by any means necessary. I must continue to offer what, in his moment of guilt, he failed to provide. Do you understand, Guillermo? The future of the Baths lies with me. And now with you, too. You have been a trusted member of this staff for nearly twenty years, and I have seen the love you have for this place. Please do not let it fall to ruin. Help me do what needs to be done."

I stopped speaking to let my words sink in. For what seemed like an eternity he sat small in his chair, his eyes downcast and roving the floor. But I knew he would agree. Guillermo had been a member of the staff since I was a child, working his way up for more than thirty years. He had devoted nearly his entire life to the Bath House, staying even through hardship and pay cuts. He had seen its birth, its rise, and its fall. There was nothing he wouldn't do for this place. He and I both knew this.

Finally, he spoke.

"What do you need from me, madam?"

I unclenched my fists, not realizing that my nails had left staccato stigmata in an arc across my palms. I discretely wiped them on my napkin.

"It's not what, but whom," I began.

"You observe most of the patrons who pass through this establishment, and you have keen eyes and ears amongst the staff. I need you to identify an individual who would not be missed. Guest, staff, it matters very little at this point. And I need you to help me with certain physical labor that I cannot do alone," I glanced around secretively, though I knew the dining room was mostly empty. "And to help me keep our activities discreet."

He looked at me then, realizing what he'd agreed to. To keep the Bath House going, even in its crumbling state, was his cross to bear—a burden we shared together now. There was nothing to be done but dive headfirst into the darkness.

"There is a man on staff... Jackson, Steven Jackson, madam. He is the assistant lobby manager and I've heard from many of the maids that he is unsavory at best. But I believe it to be worse than that."

"He is fairly new to Sutton Bath House, and I've heard reports that he is not afraid to be fresh with the ladies after sipping on his flask a few too many times."

"He sounds... perfect. Thank you, Guillermo," I said, grabbing his hand resting on the drink tray. "I realize the undesirable nature of this new role. I hope you can make peace with the fact that you are working towards a greater good."

I smiled thinly at Guillermo and he back at me. As I made to stand, he came over to me to pull out my chair, visibly relieved at the familiarity of this job function.

"Shall I get your coat, madam?"

"No thank you. I believe I'll take a walk about the Bath House. But I'll meet you in the garage at half past. Have the motor car running, I'll need your assistance after I've done my part.

"Very good," he straightened in front of me as we stood stark and glowing in the golden light of the afternoon sun. I left the grandly lit dining room and retreated into the cool interior of the bath house, the smell of saltwater clearing my head.

It was easy enough to find Steven Jackson. His favorite hiding spot was just outside a fire exit off the north side of the Bath House, down a long stretch of hallway. It was just out of sight to our guests, and yet still close enough to slip back to the front desk "unnoticed" after his bi-hourly cigarette breaks.

"Miss Sutton!" He startled when I stepped through the door, stamping out his cigarette in a fluster. "I was just heading inside for—"

"Have a light?" I asked, taking away his chance at escape. I took out my gold half-shell cigarette case from a secret pocket in my loosely fitted dress. The frock was emerald green and beaded, my favorite swanky flapper style dress. It was outdated by that time, but I loved it so. Such a shame it couldn't be salvaged.

"Of course," Jackson said, pulling out his monogrammed lighter.

"Thank you. Lovely evening, no?"

"Beautiful." He side-eyed me warily.

"I used to love watching the mountains at this time of night with my father. He had the most stunning view from his apartment windows. In fact, the light was much like this the day he died."

"Oh?" Jackson commented, his interest piqued as he turned towards me, tall and broad-shouldered as he leaned against the wall.

"He would play my favorite songs on the gramophone..." I rambled on, slipping a nonchalant hand into my pocket, my fingers searching nimbly for my small flask.

"... and that's when I knew I simply adored jazz! Couldn't get enough. Gin?"

Unscrewing the cap of my tarnished silver flask, I held it out to him. I watched his gaze trace the crescent moon engraved on its front. It was something I only carried with me but once a year.

"I really should be... oh what the heck," he said cheerfully, taking it from me and downing his first swig. The flask was small, and it wasn't enough to get him ossified, but the amount of arsenic I slipped in should drop him in a quarter of an hour.

"So... where you from? I hear you're a real cake-eater with the girls," I chatted, watching him take another sip.

"I do alright with the dolls. I don't get too handsy or nothin', but I like to show 'em a good time, or at least I did back home in Los Angeles..." He was clearly used to dominating the conversation.

And so, I waited.

The woman in the full tartan skirt tip-toes across the narrow cement walkway between the two pools. Her beau steadies her, firm hands grasping her waist from behind, as she holds her arms outstretched for balance. I watch them lose their balance for one windswept moment, tipping sideways toward the murky seawater resting dormant in the stagnant pool. They caught themselves and steadied, laughing.

"Let's go for a hot chocolate," I hear him say as they reach the other side. Their voices carry over the gusts of sea air. "I think I saw a diner down the road."

"I'm more in the mood for a malt, but that sounds swell," she replies, heading the long way around the pool toward the highway. I watch them drive away in a breezer, her hair pulled under a scarf, merging with a line of similar green and red and turquoise motor cars on their journey down the mountainside.

I make my way over to the still pool, careful not to get too close. Years of weather and tide have eroded the depth from ten feet to four, sending them back to nature and transforming once Olympic-sized pools into shallow tidepools. The water is brackish and dark but reflective. I inch closer, adjusting my eyes to see through the mirrored gray sky down into what lies beneath. The swaying seaweed carpet catches my eye at the bottom, gracefully floating in the muck and sand below.

A yellow and red candy wrapper drifts toward the surface. I shake my head and kneel down to rescue the pool from the "Bit-O-Honey" that contaminates it.

In that instant a child's face rips through the seaweed as I reach into the water, his eyes milky white and his mouth open in a soundless scream. The right side of his skull has caved in, and slimy seaweed tendrils wave at me from the hollow left behind. He launches upwards towards the surface, a grey decaying hand extending violently from the shallows to grab at mine and pull me under.

"Help… me…" he gurgles, muffled by the muck and debris that spew from his mouth and form a murky cloud, obscuring my view of him for a moment. I pull away quickly, yelping in surprise and falling backwards into the sandy dust. I clutch a cold hand to my chest and wait for the dead child to break the surface, but the water soon quiets in slow ripples.

When it's safe to close my eyes, I take a moment to catch my breath on the ground. If the echoes are stirring, it can only mean that the Watchers are near. Since those who wronged Them cannot provide offerings anymore, They must feed on the souls that have remained behind, trapped inside the trauma of the past. Those souls had no idea about the Watchers in life, so in death they can't see what comes for them on this day each year.

But perhaps this time I can make it right.

I remember waking up in the shadow of the Bath House, my dress torn around my knees and dust lining my throat. I brought my hand up to my head tenderly, but the sticky crust of dried blood on my fingertips clotted my memory. I could only guess that once he'd realized it wasn't food poisoning, he'd tried to hurt me—to punish me for his deadly mistake. The sun was wading up to its midsection in the horizon. I'm not sure how long I've been lying unconscious out here, but it can't have been for more than an hour.

I sniffed the air—vomit and sea spray threaded the breeze. Sure enough, as I gingerly sat up, I observed lumpy splatters on the ground a few feet away. Jackson's bile-drenched body slumped limply against the door.

As I dragged myself over to Jackson, I calculated how I might search for Guillermo quickly without drawing attention to my disheveled state. It would be difficult for us to drag the body to the trunk of my motor car unnoticed, but not impossible. Suddenly, something terrible and unexpected knocked the wind from my chest.

Jackson is still breathing.

I glanced up at the mountains. They were a horrifying vermillion, the same hue that silhouetted my father as he died. In that moment I knew it was already too late. There was no time to finish the job and deliver it too. I had no offering.

Panicked, scraped and bleeding, I hauled myself to my feet, wracking my brain for some way to provide the necessary sacrifice in time. It was then, as I braced against the wall to reach the door, that something bright and small caught my eye in the distance on the mountainside. Then another… and another… dotting the field of my peripheral vision on the reddening mountainside. I couldn't look, but I knew. I felt as if I were tumbling underneath the rushing tide, cold filling my lungs.

I felt their eyes on me.

I fled limping, pain be damned, through the heavy metal door and back into the side lobby. They wanted their sacrifice now. And my failure following that of my father's only meant a greater tragedy was in store for me.

I stumbled—dress tattered, legs pocked with sandy gravel, head crusted in blackish ooze—down the side hallway and into the main lobby toward the front desk.

"Madam!" exclaimed the concierge from behind the counter as I hit it with my full momentum. "Are you alri—"

"*Out!* I need all of the guests out of the Bath House. I need you to evacuate the guests immediately, *now*." He stared at me in shock, guests glancing over as they passed. The concierge staff gathered behind him.

"Is there an emergency, madam? A fire?"

"*No.* No, They're nearly here."

"Let me call for help, the house doctor passed by not a minute or two ago…"

My staff thought I had finally snapped, and who could blame them? No doubt I looked like a madwoman, but I hadn't time to waste. I whirled around and pushed off the desk, hobbling urgently through the grand lobby and down the main hall. Guests parted in alarm or indignance as I made my way, the oppressive humidity of the pools growing strong and salty as I neared. It was like the ocean had evaporated into a fine mist, and I was suffocating in it.

As I emerged from the dark hall, the main bath house lit in the last light of the red sinking sun. There were fewer guests now than in the Bath House's hay day, but there was still a crowd during peak season. The chamber echoed with shouts and splashes and joyful shrieks of children as parents swam nearby or watched from the surrounding benches. I stood at the top of the grand iron staircase, observing my kingdom with wild eyes, poised to sound the alarm at the top of my lungs. I gazed down at the pools and the swimmers below, and my voice caught in my throat.

The Watchers stood in the water, still as headstones.

They had taken a shadowy imitative form of swimmers—men and children alike—dressed in striped bathing costumes or swimming caps. A camouflage to all who did not look directly at Them, but tinted in a spectral grey darkness. They gazed up at me as the bathers continued to splash and play around Them—oblivious to the inhuman impostors in their midst. All sound faded into a tinny whine as their gaze tilted towards me in eerie synchronicity. Those bright beacon eyes stared into mine, transferring images of the future into me, like flashbulb memories going off in quick succession. I knew what was to come next.

The world slowed down as the first metal beam fell into the pool below, crushing a handful of people in its path. A stunned silence fell over the bathers. But when the sounds of the splash subsided, Hell broke loose.

Shrieks echoed hauntingly throughout the magnificent Bath House. Blood inked through the darkening waters of the pool, spreading further with each choppy wave that sloshed against the sides. I looked up into the rafters just in time to see the next beam groan and jerk to life. Its tail end hit the catwalk to my left, sending some bathers into the churning waters and others careening broken onto the concrete floor.

It was pandemonium, but my feet were rooted to the spot as I leaned on the stair railing, clutching it with all my strength. Frenzied guests fled in a stampede up the stairs, scrambling past me. I watched as a young mother held her baby to her breast in one hand, using the other to pull herself along the railing. Slipping suddenly on a slick stair, her momentum sent them both plunging forward into the ascending steps, and the child's cries of alarm went silent. Her face contorted in a wail of pain, the young woman sat on the steps cradling the lifeless bleeding babe. Her anguish soon vanished as she was trampled to a pulp underneath the panicked mob.

I looked away from this sickening sight only to watch the precarious beam fall completely, crushing a handful of terrified swimmers running to safety. It pinned four or five others to the concrete, their screams of agony out-piercing even the shrieks of the terrified survivors.

All the while, the Watchers stood stock-still in the turbulent waters as bodies and debris sloshed around Them. I knew that They would watch me while the entire building came down around us, taking as many innocent offerings as it could with it. And I would go down with my father's ship.

A profound rumbling from above moved through my bones and deep into the foundations of the Sutton Bath House. Distant cries and deafening crashes told me that the upper floors of the hotel were collapsing. The crystal chandelier in the dining room shattered under the falling ceiling. Dust and debris and metal supports came down all around me, and the Sutton Bath House buckled and groaned in its final death throes.

"Madam!" I heard a deep voice behind me yell. It was Guillermo, limping down the hallway through the crush of terrified mothers and children and families going in the opposite direction.

"Madam I waited for you, where have you been? The whole building is collapsing!" he gasped at me, taking me firmly by the elbow in an attempt to guide me to safety to the lobby. But there was no safety.

I looked at him blankly. *This is my fate.*

Suddenly, the glass walls shattered inward in one explosive burst. Shrapnel and shards sliced the air towards me, catching the light in a million tiny red sunsets. The larger pieces impaled a few guests to the back wall below me.

Fragments of metal frame and glass slivers sliced through my exposed skin in countless razor cuts.

Guillermo stumbled backwards from the force of the explosion and he looked down. A long piece of glass the length of a liquor bottle had impaled his left shoulder. He shifted in shocked indecision, his hand flitting to and from the shard as he tried to make sense of his situation.

"Go Guillermo, go get help. You must save yourself now, I am not going with you. Get out!"

My shouts brought him back to the present, and desperation filled his eyes as shock became pain.

"Please madam…" he feebly called, using his good arm to steady himself against the wall.

"*Go!*" I screamed once more over the din of falling metal and debris. But as he fled into the shadows of the hall, the ceiling finally succumbed to collapse. I couldn't see how far the cave-in had reached, but there was nothing I could do. Not for myself or for Guillermo or for my guests who had brought such joy to this place. To the home that brought me agency and independence and life. There was only chaos now, and we were only offerings.

I sank to my knees at the top of the stairs, still clutching the rail above me, and watched the last sliver of light dowse itself in the dark waters of the Pacific. And amid the last of the trapped guests escaping bloody and wounded through the shattered windows, the Watchers stood—powerful in their stillness.

And as the entire structure collapsed above me, the Watchers dissolved from view in that same smoky way I'd glimpsed when my father passed. I remember thinking that I too would surely dissolve into nothingness and disappear from all memory.

Until I woke up here.

There is an elderly man sitting on my bench. He doesn't acknowledge me as I sit, and we both stare out onto the San Cicaro coastline for a while. The lighthouse beam grows brighter as the sky turns a darker gray in the emerging dusk. It's a beautiful view and I will miss it.

"I enjoy days like this," he finally says to me, clasping his hands in his lap. He has excellent posture and a beautiful dark suit. "Gray and pure, when the wind is high but there is no storm to be seen. On days like this, time is heavier. The gray weighs everything down. It seems that there is only memory on these days. Only the past."

He turns to me, dust speckling his trimly groomed mustache.

"Do you know what day it is?" he asks.

"Yes," I reply. My heart pulls in my chest.

"Today is never a good day."

I look into his eyes, his pure and unexpected acknowledgment takes me aback. It's the first warmth I've felt in a long, long time.

"And do you, daughter, remember the letter I left for you?"

"Yes," I say, shocked. "Father, you recognize m—?"

"Of course, my little love," he exhales, his hand rising to stroke the place where my cheek would be. "And now it's time you knew the truth. It's time I end this."

I look blankly at him, confused as much by his words as by this sudden divergence in the routine. He shifts his body towards mine on the bench and takes my hand.

"When I was a young man, I had lofty beautiful dreams, as most young men do. Dreams of wealth and power and luxury, of gold and silver and steel. Dreams of holding the universe in my hand—swirling and full of life like a rippling tidepool. I worked and fought tooth and nail for these dreams and found that suddenly my dreams had turned into a vicious, horrifying reality. I had stopped at nothing to bring them to fruition, ignored all the warnings and affronts to morality. And to that end it cost me everything. But worst of all, it cost you everything."

"I… I don't understand what you mean," I articulated carefully, words nearly catching in my throat.

"When I first put plans for the Bath House into motion, I ran wildly through a maze of opposition, facing dead ends at every turn. Conservationists, politicians, investors, union men. They had sited labor risks, warned against competing with local business rivals and stirring up muck. Geologists advised against such large construction on unsteady coastal land, susceptible to all manner of disasters—everything from landslides to unusual tectonic shifts. It was a fool's errand to continue this project.

"And yet," he paused to take in the coastline, gazing at all that has changed, before turning back to me. "We broke ground anyway."

"Father…" I tried, but my voice failed me.

"Disaster abounded from day one. Floods, storms, landslides, small quakes. We were weeks behind schedule almost immediately. But it took twelve deaths within the first three months—and the resulting coverups—for me to fully grasp that I had made a grave mistake. Unseasonable rainstorms led to mudslide casualties, and gruesome job site accidents got the local men whispering about curses and doom. Some reported seeing tall creatures with bright eyes lurking on the cliffside just before each incident. I considered their stories rubbish until I finally saw Them too, over the mangled body of a worker who had fallen from the scaffold after-hours. The Watchers."

As the last syllable escaped his lips, I felt the pinprick of Their presence in the distance. The last light was fading, and the Watchers were coming as if called.

"It was then that I approached Them. I crawled toward Them through nails and gravel and mud, pleading in choked desperation to let my Bath House live. I begged Them to keep these tragedies at bay and spare my workers. They finally agreed in their silent way, and I saw the price of our bargain in my mind's eye: one life per year. Preventing the tragedies was impossible. They were inevitable, as is the nature of death and destruction. This deal only deferred them—kicked them down the road. I would have my Bath House so long as I paid in the blood of just one soul per year instead of many, compounding a debt of unspeakable interest. And one day, when I failed to continue payment, the disasters I postponed for so many decades would erupt in unknowable mayhem. That's how the Watchers would come to collect."

He glances around us for the first time then, his elegant posture wilting as we observe the echoes emerging from the ether. They are splashing and diving and running along the edges of the ruined pools. A few are joyful and at play, while others scream and flee from an invisible scene of turmoil and horror—a ghostly tableau of their final moments. I turn back to my father.

"After so many years of sacrifice and blood, I could do it no longer," he pleads beseechingly, taking my other hand and sliding closer. "I thought stupidly that my death would wash the blood from my hands, bring me peace. And so I took the coward's way out. But I was too ashamed to tell you the truth, to tell you what I had done… to tell you what monstrous debt I had accrued for so many years. My sacrifice meant that you and the Bath House would live another day, but it only placed my bloody mantle on your shoulders."

He paused then, eyes boring into mine, shimmering translucent and wet in the growing fog.

"Daughter, I am so ashamed…"

I wish now more than ever to have the ability to weep. But when you're pure spirit and emotion, there is no physical release. It only fuels itself and burns hotter, intensifying your presence here on earth.

My father was right. The gray twilight does indeed feel heavy and claustrophobic.

Suddenly, I feel the wary intensity of being observed. The Watchers are close now, drifting nearer to us with each passing minute across the cliffs from the mountains.

I look back, caught in Their intense gaze. Their eyes shine like beacons in the growing dark, seven or eight figures closing the gap between us. After years of running, manifesting in and out of time with each anniversary, I am ready. Ready to be taken. Ready to let go and to let these souls be at peace. And, somehow, I'm ready to forgive the one soul I love the most. A soul scorched and marred with guilt even in death. A soul whose dream I once shared.

The Watchers appear directly above us, looming sentinel-like in the silence. And I notice for the first time that their bright gaze feels peaceful to me. Like going home.

"Perhaps it's time we end this," I say to my father, squeezing his hands and bracing myself for the permanent dark. "Together."

Los Vigilantes Oscuros

Three plates of microfilm later, and Olivia was *still* thinking about the bath house disaster.

She couldn't help it. She never knew it even existed, and kept pondering how the bath house's final guests had died. A day where they were supposed to have fun and relax, and instead their lives were snapped up in an instant.

Nor was there ever a satisfactory explanation as to *why* it happened. Mechanical failure? Damage caused by tremors or an earthquake? Mismanagement? Maybe some combination of all three?

She went back and read the second half of the story carefully. Of note were the curious statements by a few survivors who, by chance, had been on the road to the bath house when the fiasco occured. A few had claimed to see dozens of men on the hills, simply watching the horror unfold without doing anything. By the time the bath house was gone, they were as well.

She had heard something about this once. It was a tale her friend's *abuelita* had once told her.

"*Los Vigilantes Oscuros*," she had said. "You sometimes call them 'the Dark Watchers.'"

Lost in her thoughts, Olivia almost missed the headline that zipped by her gaze. Panicking, she aborted the scan by hitting the "Ctrl" and "C" buttons, before scrolling back.

"Civilian Conservation Corps Seeks Lost Man," she read aloud. She almost thought she had wasted her time, until she noticed the words "park" and "trails."

Olivia knew those paths. She had hiked there a few times in college with her then-boyfriend, on their way into the mountains. Feeling a chill from the coincidence, she decided to read on.

Slivers

L.M. Charbonneau

The railroad bull threw Cal out of the open boxcar. He landed heavily on the dusty ground and lay still on his stomach, gasping for air, as the train rattled past. When he could breathe again, Cal rolled over carefully and sat up to take stock of his injuries. One eye was swollen, his lip was cut open, his skin would be colorful with bruises soon, and he'd be pissing blood for a few days. It could've been worse. The bull could have dumped him in the Salinas River nearby. Or shot him. With a grunt of pain, he got to his feet, dusted himself off, and stumbled over to where the small rucksack containing his paltry belongings had landed. He stretched his back, slung the bag over one shoulder, and started walking beside the tracks. He didn't know how far along he was on the route to San Cicaro, but another train would come along sooner or later.

Cal had ridden the rails from New York to Los Angeles, thinking he'd like to be near the ocean. Yet L.A. exuded an aura of hostility, as if he was always in a sniper's crosshairs, always about to walk into an ambush. He heard about San Cicaro, up north a ways on the coast. Rumor said it was recovering from the Depression, that there might be work for a young man. But the men he shared last night's meal with weren't so encouraging.

"You don't want to go there, soldier boy," old Mac said.

Cal was huddled around a fire on the beach with a bunch of other hoboes. It was a cool December night. Mac was already wearing Cal's medal pinned to his coat, and he handed Cal the promised half plate of beans in exchange.

"Why not?" Cal asked.

"It's real strange," Mac said. "Pretty, but things happen."

"Things happen everywhere." Cal ran his finger over the plate to catch every bit of the sauce from the beans.

"Things you can't explain." Mac looked grim. "José, tell him. Tell him what you saw in the water."

José shuddered and shook his head.

"I was in San Cicaro for a while," someone else said. "Five years ago now, back in '33. I was with the CCC, building parks and such."

Cal turned. The speaker sat apart from the circle of men, nearly invisible in the dark.

"You never told us that, Bill," Mac said. "Let's hear it."

José muttered something in Spanish about not wanting to talk about that cursed city before walking off, further away from the lapping water. Bill took José's place by the fire and held out his hands to the warmth.

"We were making a trail in a nature park," he said as he stared into the flames. "It was nice, with benches and a visitor center. I was paired up with this kid from Idaho. Ernest. Everybody liked Ernest. He was sweet and quiet, and he liked to sing. He had an old guitar from somewhere and he'd play it for us after dinner. Made up his own songs. Real nice kid. Hard worker, never a bad word or complaint. But the whole time we were in San Cicaro, he had nightmares. He'd start hollering in the middle of the night like he was being murdered. Every night. No one could sleep. By the time we'd been there a few days, I was the only one who'd still sit with him at mealtimes."

Bill paused and pulled a bottle out of his coat pocket. He took a long swallow and passed it to the next man. By unspoken consent, they waited for the whiskey to make its way around the circle and back to Bill before he started speaking again.

"We were out in the woods planting saplings in a bare spot—looked like nothing had grown there for a hundred years and nothing ever would, but we figured we'd try anyway—when Ernest disappeared. He didn't go far. I found him…"

Bill stopped again and took another slug from the bottle. He held onto it this time.

"I found him in a little clearing, kneeling on the ground like he was in church. Everything was dead quiet. No birds, no insects, no wind. Nothing. And I saw this thing, this black thing, latched onto Ernest's head, like a calf feeding from its mother."

"It was eating him?" Cal asked.

Bill didn't look up.

"Not on the outside," he said. "I yelled and it scattered like rain off a dog's coat into the bushes and trees. Ernest was just fine. There wasn't a mark on him. Like nothing had happened. I thought I'd lost my mind, that I was seeing things. But Ernest slept like a baby that night."

"That don't sound so bad," Mac said after a moment of puzzled silence.

Bill drank again. "Yeah, no one complained. But something wasn't right about Ernest after that. He never sang again, and he left that guitar behind when we moved on after the park was done. He still worked hard, but you could see something in him was gone. He quit the Corps on the next job. I don't know what happened to him."

"So it… ate his mind?"

"Dunno for sure. I guess so. He never had a nightmare again. I think it ate all the bad stuff, but took some of the good stuff, too. I never talked to him about it." Bill shrugged. "If I hadn't yelled, maybe it would've taken everything out of his brain. He was sure happier afterwards, though."

"You see?" Mac said to Cal. "You don't want to go no place where things'll eat your mind right outta your head."

"Sure, Mac. I guess you're right."

The conversation moved on to other topics. Cal half-listened, as Bill's story plagued his thoughts.

The next day, Cal hopped a slow-moving Southern Pacific freight train bound for San Cicaro. For much of the trip, he enjoyed the view of the Santa Lucia mountains from the open side door, until the bull found him.

It was early dawn, and cold. The scents of pine and sagebrush suffused the air. A woodpecker hammered on a tree up in one of the canyons. Small creatures scurried through the twisty-branched bushes growing a little way from the tracks. Off in the distance, across the river and below the railroad, vultures circled. Cal walked with his hands stuck into his armpits to keep his fingers warm.

He'd been walking for an hour or so under the gradually lightening sky when an airplane approached from the south. It wasn't a dive-bomber. After all, he wasn't in Spain anymore, but *he was walking along a different road, weary and bloody after a skirmish, dust coating his skin. The trucks they followed were full of the wounded. He must have been sleepwalking, for he didn't hear the Stukas or his companions' shouts until the planes were already shrieking toward the earth and the long line of men stretched across it. He turned and saw the world exploding, thudded to the futile shelter of the open ground, hands pressed uselessly over his ears as his friends' bodies erupted. Dirt, blood and fragments of their flesh rained down on him. He could do nothing. He could hear nothing but the roaring of the Stukas' guns.*

Cal came back to the present with a gasping sob and a sore throat, as if he'd been screaming. Flat on his back, staring up at the sky. Everything was still. The plane was gone. God. It had happened again. How much time had he lost? He couldn't take this anymore. Drinking to escape the memories only made things worse. He'd gotten as far as wrapping his mouth around the muzzle of a gun, but couldn't find the nerve to pull the trigger. Maybe Bill's story was true, maybe it wasn't, but at least it had sparked a flicker of hope that there was another way out.

He picked himself up and was about to set off once more when something caught his eye. There. Up on a ridge, a tall, faceless figure, all in black. It seemed to be wearing a wide-brimmed hat and carrying a walking stick. But for all its human-like appearance, it was much too large, out of scale, so he couldn't quite work out how far away it was. It stood still and watched him. He would have dismissed it as a shadow, a trick of the eye, except that it turned and walked northwards along the ridgeline. He rubbed his eyes. Had he hit his head? When he looked up again, the figure was gone. Shaking his head, he started walking.

Disorientation set in. He was hungry, thirsty, and in pain, his ribs and back aching with every step. The vision of the strange figure on the ridge had unmoored him even further. The unexpected sight of a road intersecting with the rail tracks startled him back to reality in time to notice a plume of dust. He hurried across the road and stuck out his thumb.

A green Ford truck slowed and stopped. The dust made his eyes stream. He coughed as the passenger door opened with a creak.

"Where ya headed?"

"San Cicaro," he gasped.

"I can drop ya just outside the town. That do for ya?"

Cal nodded and started to climb in, wincing, but had to pause. A black and white Collie held its ground in the doorway, sniffing at him, before giving a final whuff and jumping into the narrow space behind the seats.

"Molly's decided you're alright," the driver said. "Come on in."

He was lean, deep-tanned and wrinkled, with long white hair under a Stetson. The inside of the truck smelled pleasantly of horses and hay.

"Name's Farley," he said.

"Clarence Miller. Cal for short."

"Well, friend, no offense, but you look like hell." Farley put the truck into gear. "I don't want to stick my nose where it don't belong, but are ya sure about goin' to San Cicaro?"

"There's something I have to do there," Cal said. "Personal business."

Farley shrugged. "You got your mind made up, I guess."

They listened to the radio, Farley humming along to "Heart and Soul." As they traveled, they passed a dilapidated sign covered in dust, bearing an arrow pointed towards the coast. "Sutton Bath House 5 miles." Cal wondered absently if it was still in operation given the state of the sign.

"You from around here?" Cal asked after they'd gone a few miles.

"Sure am. Born and raised." Farley hooked a thumb toward the rear window. "My ranch is back that-a-way."

"Go into the mountains much?"

"Not as much as I'd like. Beautiful, ain't they? Pretty wild, still."

Cal hesitated. What would the other man think of his next question?

"You ever see a real tall, black fellow? With a hat and walking stick?"

Farley gave him a sideways glance, then looked back at the road.

"A man alone out there, tired, hungry, not enough water… the mind plays tricks on him. Thought I saw a giant striding along the ridgeline once, with a stick, just like you say. But no giant could just vanish between one blink and the next, now could it?"

"Of course not," Cal mumbled.

"Now, the Indians tell stories," Farley continued. "About these dark watchers in the mountains. They don't do nuthin', mind, just watch. If you try to get close, they disappear."

"So they might be real?"

"I didn't say that. But if they are, there's no harm in 'em. That city, now, you better watch yourself there."

Cal tried to draw Farley out, but the older man shook his head. "I ain't seen none of it for myself. It's all just stories. Maybe tall tales. But I'd be careful, if I was you."

Farley woke him with a shake. Muzzily, Cal peered through the windows. Fog was settling in over a street of tall buildings.

"This isn't the edge of town," he said.

"Figured you'd probably hiked far enough for one day," Farley said awkwardly. "Brung ya into the center. Wasn't too far out of my way."

"That's mighty decent of you," Cal said. "I'm sorry for the trouble."

"Listen. You seem like a nice enough young man, and you've had a hard road. I could use another worker." Farley scribbled directions on a scrap of paper and handed it to Cal. "You need a place to stay, hitch a ride out to Farley's ranch."

Cal nodded as he accepted the note. "Thanks. I'll keep it in mind."

"Watch your back here. Find yourself a room, and don't go nowhere with nobody. If I don't see ya, have a merry Christmas."

"You too."

As the truck pulled away, Cal looked at the piece of paper. There was a dollar bill folded around it, which he tucked away in his coat pocket. It was still morning, but not far into the day. Shops weren't open yet, but he saw workers moving about inside, preparing for customers. San Cicaro looked prosperous, even in the ocean-scented fog. There were Christmas displays in the shop windows, and lights decorating the lamp posts and street signs. The marquee outside the theater said some new picture called *The Dawn Patrol* was showing. He paused to look at the poster and realized it was a war flick. No thanks.

He walked on until he found a diner. It was shabby inside, but clean. A juke box in a corner was playing "Winter Wonderland." He shook out his wet, threadbare coat and flat cap at the door. An old man slept in a corner booth at the back. A priest, dressed all in black with his white collar and a gold crucifix showing, was midway through a plate of sausage and biscuits.

"What'll it be, hon? You gonna sit down a while?"

Cal blinked. The waitress was a comfortably middle-aged blonde with sharp blue eyes that swiftly took in his thin, battered face and his loose-fitting clothes.

"I don't have much money, ma'am. If you've got any work I can do…"

She sniffed. "You don't look like you can stand up much longer, hon, never mind wash any dishes. Just go on and sit yourself down, now. Take a load off. I'll be right with you."

Cal kept his eyes down as he made his way to a table by the window. He hung up his coat and hat on the rack, then sat down with his back to the other men, facing the entrance, while setting his rucksack beside him. He dug a few coins from his trouser pocket and set them on the table, but saved Farley's dollar. If things didn't pan out today, he'd need the money for a flophouse.

"That's all I've got," he said when the waitress came by with a pot in one hand and a plate of food in the other.

"You can put that away, hon. Here you go."

She slid the plate in front of him and filled his mug. Cal gaped at the feast of eggs, hotcakes, bacon, and tomato wedges. There was even a cut-up whole orange. He wiped a shaking hand over his eyes.

"Go on, now," the waitress said quietly. "It's practically Christmas, after all. Can't let a man go hungry."

"Thank you, ma'am," he whispered.

"Merry Christmas."

She moved off to refill the priest's cup. Cal rolled up his shirt sleeves to protect the frayed cuffs and tucked in, reminding himself to eat slowly so he wouldn't get sick. He was halfway through the meal when the bell over the door rang out. He looked up and froze. Two big cops walked in, shaking damp off their rain slickers. Their eyes locked on Cal's bruised face, swept over the rucksack on the seat beside him. They sauntered over and stood beside his table, blocking any escape route.

"Can I help you, officers?" he asked.

"You got the dough to pay for that food, boy?"

Had the waitress just been playing with him? Did she call the cops? Cal's fingers curled around the coffee mug.

"It's covered," he said. "Is something wrong?"

The older, beefier cop leaned in, took a close look at the tattoo on Cal's right wrist, then straightened up. "Lincoln Battalion, huh? What's that?"

Cal didn't much like the knowing expression in the cop's eyes. He should have kept the tattoo out of sight.

"International Brigade. From the war in Spain. We were disbanded last month and sent home."

"*Home*, you say. And yet here you are, in my city, which is *not* your home, is it?" The cop scowled. "Why? What are you doing here? I'm talking to you, you godless little commie bastard."

"I bet he's here to spy on the new airplane factory," the other cop said. "Let's take him in."

"I'm not a communist," Cal said. "Or a spy."

"Oh yeah? You got a job? Anyone to vouch for you? What I heard is, all you 'volunteers' broke US law and fought for the Communists. Why they let any of you back in the country is beyond me."

"Maybe someone figured we'd need to fight the fascists here, too," Cal said coolly. "Y'know, sooner or later."

The cop's face reddened. His fingers tapped the billy club at his side.

"You trying to be *smart* with us? Engage in some *political* debate?"

"I can vouch for the young man," said a smooth voice behind him.

Cal looked over his shoulder. It was the priest, delicately wiping his lips with a napkin, who had interceded. The younger cop took a half step back. The older one's brow rose, but he stood his ground. Why either of them should be bothered by this guy was beyond Cal.

"Uh, no disrespect, *padre*, but it sure don't look like he's with you," the older cop said.

"I have been waiting for him," the priest said. "I did not realize this was my man until he mentioned his battalion."

"You harboring commies now?"

The priest did not answer, but he must have done something Cal didn't catch, because the color drained from the cops' faces.

"Okay, uh, well, *padre*, if you're willing to vouch for him, I guess that's okay."

"Then do not let me detain you any further, officers."

Cal stared, openmouthed, as the police left the diner.

"May I?" The priest nodded at the empty seat across from Cal.

"Uh, yeah, sure. Thanks… for that."

"*De nada. ¿Habla español?*"

"A little." The sound of Spanish and the feel of it in his mouth made him queasy, but there was no use trying to explain that.

The waitress materialized at the priest's elbow with a fresh cup of coffee. She refilled Cal's mug.

"Can I get you anything else?"

"Just the bill, please, my dear," the priest said. "And breakfast for Frank back there, when he wakes up."

The priest was medium-sized, well-built for a man of the cloth, with powerful shoulders and a lean face. It was difficult to guess his age. Fifty, maybe? His accent was different from what Cal had become accustomed to in Spain. Maybe Mexican. Something about him was odd, but Cal couldn't focus enough to decide what it was. His gaze fixed on the gleam of the crucifix, and then he was back *in some Spanish town he'd never learned the name of, watching anarchists drag a wailing priest from his church. His face was already a mask of blood. The other anarchists waiting in the street didn't bother questioning him. Someone had reported that he supported Franco's Nationalists, and that was enough. The commanding officer cocked his pistol, walked up to the priest, and shot him between the eyes. The last clinging tendrils of Cal's faith in a higher power died with the priest. The remaining fighters jogged from the church as flames began to lick at the windows from the inside.*

Cal blinked and looked away. A swig of coffee washed the taste of bile from his throat. The waitress came by and left the priest's bill, then disappeared into the kitchen.

"My name is Father Andreas," the priest said. "I lead the San Cicaro Mission. I apologize for the rude treatment."

"I'm Cal. I'm really not a communist or a spy."

"It would not matter one bit to me if you were, my son. The policeman also called you 'godless,' and I cannot help noticing you did not deny that."

"I'm also not a liar," Cal said. "And you can save your breath if you were thinking about preaching at me."

Andreas smiled. "I would not presume. But what has brought you to our city?"

"Just some personal business."

"You have family here?"

"No. I'm not from San Cicaro. I was here with the CCC in '33. We built a nature park. I decided to come back and see if there was any work." Cal figured he was safe in borrowing Bill's story.

Andreas rested his elbows on the table and steepled his fingers under his chin. "What was it about San Cicaro that drew you back? The city was not at its best in, when was it? 1933? In fact, I seem to recall some trouble afflicting the CCC during its time here."

"I don't know what you're talking about," Cal said. "We came, we built the parks, we left."

"Ah well, perhaps I am mistaken. So many unfortunate things have happened that it is easy to become confused."

"I guess so." Cal finished the last bite of bacon and set his fork down. "I don't mean to be rude, Father, but I should get going."

"Where are you going? I would not normally pry, but as you have seen, the police here are not welcoming, and they will be watching you. You are injured. And I sense you are troubled. Perhaps I can help."

"That's a real prize-winning deduction, Father. A young man comes back from war, broke and beaten up, and you figure out he's got problems."

Andreas spread his hands. "If you need a bed, you are welcome at the Mission."

Cal shook his head. "Thanks, but I'll make my own way."

"I shall pray for you, then."

"Sure." Like Cal could stop him. "See you around."

Cal collected his coat, cap and rucksack, then left the priest at the table. He gave the waitress a wave in thanks, and stepped outside into the heavy fog. The city was stirring now. Shops were opening, their lights like bright islands in the gloom. The headlamps of the occasional car driving down the street sliced through the murk. Cal shivered and looked back over his shoulder once or twice. He was sure someone was following him, but if so, he couldn't see the pursuer. Anyway, what could they do to him that Spain hadn't already tried?

After asking directions a couple of times, he found his way to the park entrance. A breeze rose, and the fog lifted enough for him to see a little way into the forest. The trees loomed high above, their crowns forming an interlaced canopy, with the exception of a magnificent oak that somehow towered over the rest. Not much light would have gotten through even on a sunny day, and it sure wasn't one of those. He hesitated, then took the trail towards the visitor center. The sounds of the city disappeared, replaced by the chirping of sparrows and finches, and the creaking of the trees as they swayed. The trail was soft beneath his boots. He'd never been in a real forest before, and its immensity and complexity made him feel insignificant. He walked quietly and breathed in the heady smells of wet leaves, bark, and earth.

There was a clearing a little way off the trail, with a wooden bench. He pushed through the ferny undergrowth, sucking droplets of clean-tasting water off his hands as he went. He brushed off the bench, folded his coat around himself, and sat down. He hadn't realized how tired and sore he was until he rested. He fought the urge to sleep, wishing he had a cigarette to keep him awake. He removed his cap, shook it out, and set it on his knee, then combed his fingers through his damp hair. Birds sang and chirped all around the clearing.

Well, what had he expected? That the black thing would be waiting for him? Maybe he needed to advertise, or something. Broadcast his bad memories, like a radio show.

He took a deep breath, closed his eyes, and recalled crossing *into Spain over the Pyrenees with a group of other new volunteers. Late January, 1937. They waited until dark to avoid border patrols, then followed their local guide up and up and up, single file on the narrow, slick, treacherous trails. They shivered and shook with the cold. There was deep snow. Cal was holding the hand of the man ahead when he felt a jerk, stumbled forward, and lost his grip. There was a curse, a splash, a despairing cry. The other man had fallen into one of the mountain streams. They somehow got him out and back up onto the trail. But his leg was broken, and he was soaked through and freezing. They debated, through whispers up and down the line, whether to bring him or leave him. The injured man pleaded with them not to abandon him. The guide said he'd return the next day.*

They all knew it would be too late by then.

Cal left with the others anyway.

He opened his eyes. Nothing. The clearing looked the same. Birds still sang. His offering wasn't enough. He'd been cowardly, shying away from the worst memories. He looked up at the trees overhead. He didn't want to think about these things. But he needed to draw the black thing to him.

Chew on this, he thought bleakly, and remembered *marching through a bombed-out town, smoke still rising from the collapsed buildings, the eye-watering reek of shredded bodies in the street. Shattered glass crunching under their boots. Crows tugging at a dead horse's belly. A cringing dog crawled from the rubble with a child's foot in its mouth. Cal shot it*, and came back to the present with a ragged gasp.

There was no sound in the clearing besides his own heavy breathing.

Oh.

The blackness flowed toward him from the shadows like ink rolling through water. It was strangely beautiful, its movement tentative, like that of a skittish wild animal. He offered up another memory, of the small, frozen form of a starved girl in Teruel. The thing rippled a little closer.

Pinned down in the heat of the Ebro Plain. Nationalist guns shattered the tall rocks that Cal and his team were using for cover. The shards became flying shrapnel...

The blackness was swirling around his head, a fraction of a space away from touching him. Cal closed his eyes. He was ready.

Please, he thought. *Take it from me. Take all of it.*

There was a moment of utter stillness and calm. Then it was cracked open by a voice behind him declaiming something in a strange language, shocking the thing into a thousand midnight pieces. He twisted around and got up onto one knee, the hair on the back of his neck standing on end.

It was the priest, Father Andreas, in his black clothes and coat, standing there with his arms raised. A nimbus of blinding, unearthly light surrounded him as he shouted with an almost inhuman voice. The black thing fled from the clearing.

Andreas stopped speaking, and the light vanished. Cal remembered to breathe. The priest came closer and held out a hand.

"Come, my son. You are safe now."

Cal lunged and managed to get in a punch before Andreas gripped his wrists and held him still.

"You bastard!" Cal raged. "You fucking bastard!"

He struggled to get free, but Andreas was too strong. He collapsed to his knees and wept. Andreas knelt and put an arm around his shoulders.

Whatever the priest whispered turned the world inside out. Cal emptied his stomach on the flagstones beneath him. A bell was ringing. The green smells of the forest had been replaced abruptly, impossibly, by the scents of the city and the ocean. Dazed, Cal finally managed to look around. The forest was gone. He was kneeling in the courtyard of an old, Spanish-style church with a white bell tower. Andreas stood beside him, dusting off his trousers and coat. This was obviously the Mission. How had they gotten there? Had he blacked out again?

Andreas bent down and helped Cal up with a hand under his elbow. "Come. I will explain everything inside."

He went without resistance. The fog still lingered, blurring the edges of the courtyard, obscuring the trees and shrubs that lined it. Andreas led him up a wide set of steps to a pair of heavy, black wooden doors which opened at a touch. The ringing bell stopped as Cal crossed the threshold. The church was dark inside, despite the whitewashed walls and windows. A pair of unlit chandeliers hung from the exposed roof beams over the empty pews. The altar was in a recessed alcove, flanked by statues of Jesus and Mary. Between the windows along the walls, there were other statues that Cal assumed were the usual saints, even though the heads seemed misshapen.

It's the shadows, he told himself. *From all those votive candles around them.*

Strangely, there were no signs that it was the day before Christmas. It had been years since Cal last attended a Midnight Mass, but he remembered what a church should look like.

"This way," Andreas said. "We will be more comfortable in my residence."

Cal followed the priest through several doors and rooms until at last they reached a study furnished with two leather armchairs and a desk. There were shelves crammed with books that looked and smelled ancient. He was so tired that the titles on the spines seemed to blur and move, as if they did not want him to read them. One shelf held glass jars and bottles of various sizes that contained preserved eyeballs, claws, and other, unidentifiable pieces of what he hoped were animals. In one corner stood a full suit of armor. He wasn't certain in the dim light from the single window, but it looked an awful lot like what the conquistadors wore. Andreas caught him peering at it.

"I was not always a priest," he said.

"But that was hundreds of years ago…" Cal stopped as, with a complicated gesture, Andreas ignited the logs laid in the fireplace without touching anything.

The priest took one of the armchairs.

"Ah, that is better. Please, sit down. You look as if you are about to faint."

"How did you do that?"

"Do sit, Cal. You are tired and have had a shock. I will explain."

Cal sank into the chair, clutching the armrests. He wanted to believe he was dreaming, but the black thing had been real. Hadn't it? Or had he finally, truly lost his mind?

"You are neither dreaming nor insane," Andreas said. "And no, I am not reading your mind. I merely have experience of what it is like to learn that the world is not as one thought."

"Are you even a real priest?"

"I am fully ordained in the Catholic priesthood. And this Mission does serve the less fortunate of the city. But I confess that my methods are unorthodox. That is why I am here, in this obscure place, out of the way and beneath the notice of my superiors."

"Back there in the forest, it looked like you used… magic. And just now, to light the fire." It cost Cal to say that out loud, and he winced at his own foolishness. Surely Andreas would laugh and deny it?

"I did."

"What?"

"I did, indeed, use magic. I also used magic to bring us here." Andreas gestured at the books. "I have studied the occult arts for a very long time. And yes, that armor was mine."

"That's… impossible."

"Imagine my surprise when I did not grow old and die like my companions! I still do not know why, despite my research." He shook his head with a smile. "I would be a rich man if I knew how to share that gift with others."

Cal forced himself to take a deep breath. Nothing Andreas said or did should be possible in a world that made sense, but he'd decided during the war that expecting things to make sense was futile. He was way out of his depth, and he really only needed to understand one thing. "Why did you stop me?"

"If you saw a man about to throw himself from a bridge, would you not try to prevent him?"

"I might guess he had a good reason," Cal said. "I didn't ask you to interfere. You had no right!"

Andreas leaned forward, the leather chair creaking as his weight shifted. "I do not believe you truly wish to end your life. You could have done so many times over by now. It is not difficult to find death in battle."

"What the hell do you know about what I want?" No, death—physical death—wasn't his goal. He didn't want to be himself anymore. That was the problem he hoped the creature would solve, not that he was going to offer that up to Andreas.

"Do you think you are the only man to be haunted by what he has witnessed? To have to bear festering slivers of memory? *I helped murder a civilization.* I, too, once thought the soul-eater could be used to ease pain. But it is a menace. It senses unhappiness and it stalks its unfortunate victims through the city. Then it steals their souls—their minds, if you prefer—from them. You cannot control what it takes from you. I have been hunting it for a long time."

He was sure happier afterwards, though, Bill's words echoed in Cal's mind.

"So why didn't you catch it just now? You had your chance."

"I was unprepared." Andreas sat back again. "My first instinct was simply to drive it away from you and bring you here, to safety."

Cal had a feeling Andreas was building up to something and also holding a lot back, like one of the political officers seeking volunteers for some asinine assault. "Look, just cut to the chase. What do you want?"

Andreas smiled. "You want the soul-eater to take away your bad memories, yes?"

"Yeah."

"Then I propose that we work together. The creature knows me well, from my previous attempts to capture it. It will not come to me, no matter how many nightmares I offer it. But if you draw it in…"

"You want to use me as bait."

"In a nutshell, yes."

"What makes you think it will come to me again, after you scared it off?"

Andreas spread his hands. "There is no way to be certain, except to try. I will keep my distance until the soul-eater is… occupied… with you. What do you have to lose?"

"Fine," Cal said. "I'll do it. But you need to give it time to work on me. I don't know how you'll figure that out, but I came to this city for one reason. You can do what you want with the thing after that's done."

"Agreed." Andreas stood. "To save time, I will send us back to the clearing. That will be easier from outside, in the garden."

"No time like the present, huh?" Cal muttered as he followed the other man.

Andreas led him through different rooms to a surprisingly large walled garden. Weak sunlight shone on untidy shrubs, their dark foliage in need of pruning. A few apple trees reached out with long, twisted limbs. Cal wouldn't have eaten one of those apples for anything. In the center of the garden stood a roofed enclosure made up of several barred cages. The stench coming from them made Cal cover his mouth and nose, but he could not help going closer to see what was inside.

A morose raven with two heads clacked its beaks and shuffled to the back of its cramped cage. A wolflike animal with paws like hands lay panting on its side in another box, ribs showing through scarred skin and patchy fur. In a third cage, a tiny, winged humanoid creature hunched over itself. It raised its head and stared back at Cal with dull insectoid eyes.

"My God..." he breathed.

"Do not waste your pity on my specimens," Andreas said. "They are serving their purpose."

Cal shuddered. When this was done, he never wanted to see the priest or his Mission again.

"Let get this over with," he said.

Andreas put his hand on Cal's elbow and spoke the terrible words again.

Cal thought he was prepared this time, but still ended up retching on the grass. Even Andreas looked pale. Violating the physical laws of the universe must take it out of a man.

"I will leave you alone now," Andreas said, his voice weak. "I will not be far away."

"Fine." Cal was relieved as the priest left. He had to resist the temptation to run. After all, he could always come back tomorrow or the day after, once he was sure Andreas had lost track of him. But what if the priest was right? What if the soul-eater would gorge on more than Cal bargained for?

Cal shook his head and looked to the sky, unsure of the time. About noon, maybe. It seemed as if days had passed instead of hours since he arrived in San Cicaro. He stretched out on his back, ignoring the dampness of the ground, and stared up at the waving treetops and branches scudding across the sky. Unbidden, he recalled flying a kite in Central Park with his father. He would have been about ten years old. He pushed that memory aside. The soul-eater wouldn't be interested. What it needed was *his first battle, at Jarama. Assaulting a machine gun position with bayonets. Hundreds of brand-new comrades dead in the mud. Crawling back to their position through driving rain. Crawling over pieces of bodies. His hand stuck inside someone else's bone and flesh after he set it down in their ripped-open face.*

Not enough, even though tears flowed and nausea threatened him again.

Alone, waiting for a monster to rip my memories from my head, he thought. *What a way to spend Christmas Eve.*

And then the floodgates opened, and he was drowning in family holidays and school and neighborhood friends, all of whom he'd lost either by leaving them behind in New York or burying them in Spanish soil.

The forest was quiet. He sat up, wiping his face. The creature was hesitant, a rippling shadow among the trees.

"Come on, then," he whispered. "Come on, you bastard."

Eyes closed, he reached past the horrors of the war to the deepest wound, the one he could hardly bear to touch.

Dinner at his parents' house. His sister across the table, eyes wide as he explained his convictions, his plans. He was leaving college. In the morning, he would take a ship across the ocean to Paris, and then travel to Spain, to do his part against the fascist Nationalists. It seemed so right, so obvious that he had to do this thing. Mother wept. And Father laughed at first.

"Don't be a bloody fool," he said, his English accent sharpened by scorn. "You've no idea what being a soldier means. It's not glory and honor, I'll tell you that."

"This fight's different."

"God help us, I suppose you think your new friends are telling you the truth, and it'll all be flag-waving and camaraderie and heroism. Idiocy. You're just another lamb to the slaughter. You'll desert or be dead in a week." His father began to wheeze.

"You survived."

The wheeze turned into the familiar hacking cough Cal had heard all his life.

"You know damned well I got gassed and wasn't fit to return to the war, you insolent little sod," Father said when he could speak again. "Go on, then. You think you're better than us? Go and see for yourself. You can clear out now. And if by some miracle you do survive, don't come back here."

Cal found himself cast out on the street outside his home, with his rucksack and a gold watch stolen from his father's dressing table drawer.

The soul-eater was close now, its presence raising the hairs on his arms and neck.

Back home from the war, fresh off the ship in New York. He knocked on the door of his parents' house. Father answered. Took one look and shut the door in his face. Cal pounded on the door, screamed for his mother, his sister. No one came. Strangers stared. At last, he turned away and found a pawn shop where he could sell the watch.

He opened his eyes. The blackness surrounded him.

"I'm not afraid," he said.

He expected violence and pain. But the soul-eater's touch was like snowflakes settling on his skin. It brushed his mind as if asking permission to enter, a guest rather than an invader. It was curious, and sorrowful, and lonely. It wanted to ease his pain. Cal remembered himself as a small boy, cradling a wounded bird in his hands. He let his breath out in a sigh.

The barrage of harsh words was a painful shock. Cal screamed as the black creature tore free from his mind. He rolled on the ground, hands over his ears.

When he could bear to look up, the creature was trapped, a trembling heap beneath a glowing net. Andreas was standing over it.

"You were supposed to wait," Cal snarled as he got to his feet.

"The soul-eater is unpredictable," Andreas said. "I had to stop it before it harmed you."

"That's a load of horse shit! You never intended to follow through on your part of the deal." His hands curled into fists. "What is this thing to you anyway, just some weird butterfly for your collection? It sure doesn't seem evil to me."

Moved by an unexpected compassion, Cal crouched beside the trapped soul-eater and touched it through the net before Andreas could stop him. The creature flooded him with memories of mountains like the ones he had traveled through to San Cicaro. A sense of belonging, watching humans move through its landscape, then capture, separation, terror—and the face of the priest. Cruelty witnessed and suffered. Disintegration. An escape, finally, to a place that reminded it of home. But there were no others of its kind there, and it did not know how to return.

Andreas yanked Cal away.

"What are you doing? Do not let this thing deceive you."

Cal got to his feet.

"I don't think it's the one playing tricks," he said. "What did you do to it?"

"It belongs to me. I appreciate your assistance, but you must stand aside."

"Are you going to kill it?"

Andreas shrugged. "Eventually, perhaps. I do not yet know if it can be killed. That is one of the things I intend to find out."

Cal looked down at the creature. It had gone still, as if exhausted, and he sympathized. He had returned from Spain hollowed out, stripped of the ideals and illusions that had made him volunteer to fight. His father had been right after all, he realized bitterly. All that sacrifice, and nothing to show for it but nightmares.

He looked at the priest. One thing the war had taught him well, was to recognize monsters.

"I can't let you take it," he said to Andreas.

"Do not be a fool. Stand aside."

Cal's eyes narrowed. Any lingering doubts melted, and he stepped between the priest and the soul-eater.

Andreas sighed. "You cannot stop me. You do not understand the power I possess."

"I've faced bad odds before."

"And look where that has gotten you. Unwanted in your own country. Weak and alone."

Andreas raised his hands and began to chant again. Cal rushed forward, with no plan other than to bring the priest to the ground and subdue him before he could use his magic. He managed to grab the other man, but Andreas was too strong. The priest began some other spell, spitting the words in Cal's face. The strength of his arms evaporated, and his knees gave way. Andreas shoved him away, and he fell beside the trapped soul-eater.

"What are you gonna do, Father? Kill me, too? Isn't that against one of your commandments?"

"It is not necessary to kill you," Andreas said as he looked down. "I shall merely incapacitate you so that you cannot interfere, and I shall take the creature back to the Mission where it belongs."

The priest frowned in concentration and spoke in his magic tongue once more. Cal felt his limbs freezing in place. He struggled, but it was no use. He couldn't move. It was over. He hadn't made a lick of difference in the war, and he hadn't made a lick of difference here.

Andreas stepped closer to the soul-eater, his face distorted by an avid grin. Cal's spittle reached the hem of the priest's robe.

A thud shook the earth, and something appeared in the trees behind the priest.

The huge, dark figure walked into the clearing, banging its walking stick on the ground. It made no noise, but Cal felt the impact reverberate through his body.

Andreas wheeled to face it, hurling another spell. The dark watcher absorbed it with no apparent effect. As it moved toward the soul-eater, Andreas backed away, his arms wide.

"You… you cannot be here," he stammered. "You cannot leave the mountains."

The dark watcher ignored the priest. It bent down and tore away the net. Then it picked the soul-eater up and cradled it to its chest. Cal watched with amazement as the soul-eater began to change shape. In a few heartbeats, it stood beside its rescuer, a much smaller version with no hat or walking stick.

"It's a child…" Cal breathed. "You took a child?"

"God gave man dominion over all the creatures of the earth! They are ours to do with as we please!"

The adult watcher looked at Andreas. Then it was right in front of him. Cal would have sworn it didn't move—it was just in a different place than before. Andreas tried another spell, but it had as little effect as the first. The watcher reached a hand towards the priest.

"No!" He snarled. "Stay back, unholy beast!"

It touched Andreas on the chest, just below where the gold crucifix shone against the priest's black shirt. The priest stopped talking. His eyes widened— he tried to say something, but no words would come.

He turned and ran down the trail in terror.

The watcher turned to Cal. The young one, the soul-eater, had been hiding behind its elder. It emerged and appeared to be telling the older one something as they gazed at Cal together.

"I didn't know what he was doing," Cal said to the small one. "I hope… I hope you'll be alright. You know, some day."

Both watchers suddenly became immense. He had that same feeling he did in the mountains, of not being able to grasp how close or how far away they were.

He closed his eyes. "I don't blame you if you want to stomp on me. Just make it quick?"

Instead of bone-crushing force, he felt a gentle intrusion in his mind. He stood still while the dark watcher examined his memories, the good and the bad. He was surprised by how many of the former there were. Even Spain hadn't been entirely a nightmare. At last, he felt his pain ease, as if the watcher had drawn the poison from his mind's wounds.

When he opened his eyes again, the dark watchers were gone.

Cal stayed in the clearing for a little while, listening to the birds and poking at his memories. He remembered everything, or at least he thought he did. After all, how would he know the difference? No, it was all there, he was sure—all the horrors and all the things he was ashamed of. But he could see more clearly now, could feel justified anger and deep sorrow without losing himself. There were even moments that he might, someday, feel proud of.

Eventually, he walked back through San Cicaro. He spent a little of Farley's dollar on some coffee and a doughnut at a place by the beach where a fairground was being built. Remembering José, he stayed away from the water. It had warmed up enough now that he could take his coat off and roll up his shirt sleeves. He didn't care if anyone saw his tattoo. He wasn't staying. But there was something to do before he left.

The locks on the cages smashed easily with one of the heavy gold candle holders from the chapel. Cal hurled the broken pieces of iron away into the shrubs. After a moment's hesitation, he threw the dented candle holder back toward the chapel. Andreas was welcome to it, if he returned. There had been no sign of him when Cal arrived. He opened each cage door and stood well back.

The raven was the first to leave. It glared suspiciously until satisfied that Cal wasn't going to do anything, and then it took off with a triumphant cry. The little winged creature followed in a rush, its flight unsteady but determined. The quasi-wolf cringed and whimpered in its cage, but eventually crawled out onto the gravel path. Cal stayed very still as it sniffed the air and swiveled its pointed ears.

"¿Hola?"

Cal's heart jumped with surprise. The wolf's ears flattened and it crouched, snarling. It was Andreas, wandering into the garden and staring around as if he had no idea where he was.

"¿Hola? ¿Qué lugar es este?"

The wolf cocked its head. Before Cal could react, it sprang at Andreas and in a moment had him on the ground.

"No!" Cal shouted.

Andreas was weeping in terror, hands in front of his face. He made no other attempt to defend himself. There was no magic. The wolf was pinning him with its forepaws on his chest.

"Andreas?" Cal edged closer, keeping a wary eye on the wolf.

"¡Por favor, por favor, no dejes que me haga daño!"

The wolf sniffed Andreas all over. Cal would have sworn it looked surprised. With a snort, it gave Cal a final glance and then trotted away, leaving its captor unharmed.

Cal squatted beside Andreas. "Do you know who I am?"

He got only a blank look and more frightened begging.

He tried again, "¿Sabes quién soy?"

Andreas stared and shook his head.

I'll be damned, he thought. *The watcher must have taken away his memories.* Cal noticed some white hairs at the priest's temples that he was sure hadn't been there before. *Maybe his immortality, too.*

It was tempting to leave him to wander the city. In the end, he raided the offerings box, walked with Andreas until he was able to hail a cab, and then bundled him into the car with instructions to the driver to take him to a hospital. He got in beside the priest, pressed all the money into the cabbie's hand, and asked to be let out first, someplace he could hitch a ride out of San Cicaro.

It was early twilight when Cal hopped out of the delivery truck's cab at the Farley ranch gate. The driver honked as he pulled away. A long bungalow stood at the end of the dirt lane, with a barn and corral to one side. He heard chickens, and barking. Jazz music drifted through an open window.

An airplane passed overhead. He closed his eyes and gripped the top rail of the gate, waiting for a horror that never came. He didn't lose himself in the past, didn't end up weeping on the ground.

He opened his eyes and looked to the mountains. In the distance, a pair of dark figures blocked out the first stars as they moved purposefully across the land. He blinked and they were gone.

"I didn't get a chance to say thanks," he said quietly. "Maybe you can hear this somehow, or maybe you know how I feel from being inside my head. I hope so. Good-bye, and good luck."

Farley came out of the barn and waved, as Molly ran up the lane, tail wagging. Cal raised a hand in reply, opened the gate and stepped through.

A Break

Olivia switched focus to find any references to the Dark Watchers, using her eyes rather than her tools to scan through the headlines. She tried to recall another article she had read, by a folklorist called Dr. Walther Montgomery, who spoke a little on the subject. He never claimed they were anything sinister, as some suggested, but more like sentinels of fate… unbiased, amoral. Some called them the heralds of a new era. Olivia wondered where he got his PhD, or where exactly he was getting all this information. It's not like you could interview a Dark Watcher, could you?

Nevertheless, the idea of them wouldn't leave her head. Suddenly, Olivia wondered if she'd ever seen a Watcher. Out the corner of her eye, up on those trails. A half-glimpsed shadow, standing between the trees?

Or in the shadows of a basement.

She shivered, and pushed herself back in her chair, peering into the gloom behind her. The hair on her neck stood on end. She glanced at the phone, but thought better of it. *I need to stop freaking myself out.*

Maybe a little break was in order.

The elevator carried her back to the main lobby. Keanu looked up from helping a visitor to smile at her, which she returned. She went to the water fountain to take a sip, and wished it was cold and filtered.

Lifting her head from the spigot, she came face to face with Rosie the Riveter, forever confidently flexing on the yellow background of her poster.

The poster jarred a memory from her days in college. History of San Cicaro was one course she almost dropped out of, until the professor promised to discuss some of the city's unsolved mysteries. Such as the accident which ended the city's naval wartime production during World War II, a step back for the women who had entered the workforce.

The embers of intrigues stoked, suddenly Olivia thought of something she should check.

She swung by the front desk, where Keanu was even more eager to speak than her. "Hey, so, I'm actually about to get off early for a doctor's appointment."

"You're going to lock me out?" Olivia said, making a pouty face.

He laughed. "I mean, we *could* swap numbers if you need to call for help or anything…"

Well aren't you a smooth operator, she thought. A smile crept on her face, and she stroked some hair behind her ear. "Alright…"

The librarian whipped out his phone, and took down her number as they walked back to the elevator. As the car arrived, he texted her, and she felt the buzz of his message in her pants' pocket.

"Well this is you," he pulled the cage open and pressed the button for her. "Have fun down there."

"*By~ye,*" she sang as the door began to close, before worry pecked at her confidence. That may have been *too much* interest. Knowing this, she opted not to read the text *just* yet, so the "seen" status wouldn't appear on his end. *Yeah Olivia. That'll show him.*

She returned with a purpose, and immediately began to scan through the date-stamped cards on the storage drawers, seeking the section for the 40's. From there, it was only a matter of drilling down the year, month, and then day. With a deftness borne of experience, she soon had the article loaded on her reader, and leaned forward to read it manually.

It was a little surprising that the incident wasn't the banner headline, but rather toward the bottom of the front page. An incident too big to ignore, too weird to spotlight.

And didn't that just summarize San Cicaro in a nutshell?

Ascension of the USS Fairweather

Alex Singer

The man from the docks looked her up and down as he took another breath of his cigarette.

"Eh. She's not much, but she'll do."

Beulah Wanes heard that a lot in life.

But the pay sounded decent, so she packed it up and went. Her and all the rest of the men who'd been frozen out of peach picking for having an accent and coming from east of the border. Her Ma didn't much care, she had three other kids who could talk without slurring. Her Pa didn't care, because he was spending most of his days drunk in the shack. The collective Cousins Darling weren't around to scream at her. Gran had already died out of protest for the move.

So near sunrise that next morning, Beulah went to the drydocks. They handed her a pile of stain-grey work clothes, shoved her into an empty supply closet, and told her to just knot it over her ankles if it was too long.

She reported to the foreman. A second-tier engineer. He was a big, pink sweaty man who'd been put in charge of the girls and was mad as hell about it.

"You an Okie?" he asked, as he checked her papers and noticed the "X" she'd put instead of her name.

Beulah shook her head.

"Arkie?"

Beulah nodded, miserably. She hated the name, but it wasn't exactly untrue.

"Not a talker, huh?" There was a warning flash of white in the man's gray eyes, the silent, "You stupid, or cocky?"

"No, sir," mumbled Beulah. "Not much good at it."

"Good," said the foreman, crumpling her papers up in one hand and shoving it in the bin with the rest. "I hate girls who chatter."

So, they lined her up with the others and introduced her to the Machine.

The Machine was being made for the War. The War was being fought overseas. The engineers and the foremen, they all worked for the Navy, and everyone in the Navy wanted revenge. Someday, someday soon, the Machine would bring it, flying over the slate grey waves, a steel chariot powered by smoke and flame.

Who they wanted revenge against, Beulah wasn't sure. Probably the Japanese. No one had anything good to say about them. Everyone was convinced they'd attack again someday. Yet while the towers squalled each night as they announced another air raid drill, no one ever saw anything more than the base planes and the occasional weird triangles of light over the hills.

But that was San Cicaro for you.

The Machine was going to win the War. That's what the foremen thought, and the engineers, and then the men really working on it. The ones who banged on its hull and soldered its steel bones. They worshipped the Machine. They worshipped it with their hammers and their soldering irons and their work songs. They worshipped it with drippings from their greasy sandwiches at lunch and the whistle at the end of the day. When they lined up to punch out, and each of them banged its growing flank with a proprietary tap of their scarred knuckles. The men coming in for the night shift did the same, and so the new parishioners replaced the old.

The men all had scars from their work. Scraped knees or cracked calluses were common. Others had burns on their faces from the flying sparks or a missing finger or two from a slipped awl. That was part of their worship, too.

Calhoun was one of these men, one of the block engineers, a regular high priest of the work week. He had a face pitted in little burn scars, and a jaw hardened by the number of times he'd held a screwdriver between his teeth.

"Any of you gals know how to climb?"

Beulah and a few others raised their hands, shyly.

"Any of you know how to take a fall?"

Beulah and the other girls shook their heads.

"You'll learn," he said.

The Wanes lived in a shack in San Cicaro's last shanty town, the only place left with space for them. It used to be the old transfer station, a rich person's word for the city dump. After the junk piles started talking to people, the city had voted to move the station, and left the piles right where they were. The last Arkies and Okies to make it to San Cicaro used the garbage to build their homes. If the junk piles tried to tell them things like God was in the Desert or they had to kill the King, they didn't pay it any mind. They were too tired to do anything more than sleep when they came back from their day's work on the farms and factories.

The Wanes built their shack out of sheets, plastics, and scorched drywall. They held it together with nails they'd dug out of some child's discarded treehouse.

The boards had some weird writing that glowed when it rained, and the drywall had scratch marks from some large animal. Yet once the work was done they could fit Ma, Pa, and the three boys, while the Collective Cousins Darling slept in the jalopy. Beulah gathered what little was hers and slept on her coat in the trunk.

Ma waited by the firepit, scrubbing out the one pot they owned.

"And where you been?"

"Found some work," said Beulah. "Out on the docks. Pay's all right. Says I'll get it on the second week. If I save up, bet we can—"

But Ma held up her rag like a shield between them.

"Forget I asked," she said. "At least we had more for lunch. Stop gobbling and be of some use, yeah? Go help your brothers out by the old ice box will you? The pile took Luther's ball, and it says he won't get it back 'till he finds it a jar of eyes or something like."

Beulah went to help her brothers out by the piles. She'd just have to tell Ma when the money came in. That'd be something worth telling.

Beulah Wanes and the other girls rolled in the Machine's innards. Their smaller hands were good for reaching into the tighter spaces to check the divots and the screws and for fixing any loose wires or skipped gears. The veins and sinew that held the whole beast together. The lead girl, Mama Rose, walked them through what would one day be the Machine's lower deck—B-1, B-2, engine room, boiler room. Belly of the beast. Mama Rose was missing the tips of two fingers on her right hand, and bore a rosy scar on her left cheek. Mother superior.

She told the girls if they were lucky or if they behaved themselves, it was easy work, sliding under a plate close to the ground. If they were unlucky, they were up on the scaffolding with the true believers, checking what would one day be the beast's upper deck—its impossibly twisted spine.

The fitter, faster girls soon learned a clever trick.

"Oh, Bella said she'll go," they said to Calhoun. "She's good for that."

Beulah hadn't told them anything more than her name, but it was the first time anyone said she'd be good at something. So, she climbed the scaffolding, held her braid in her teeth, and dangled upside down while she checked the panels.

She slipped. She was always going to. She grabbed at whatever she could, catching a bar for a split second before the unfinished metal cut her and she fell like an angel. Her body went light and limp with acceptance.

She'd almost been good for something.

The world became pain and stars. The world became the beating in her head and the voice of the Machine.

Hear me, hear me, hear me.

Then her eyes were open and she was staring up into the approving faces of Mama Rose and Father Calhoun.

"How many fingers am I missing?" asked Mama Rose.

Beulah shakily held up two fingers. Father Calhoun and Mama Rose exchanged looks.

"Not bad for a first," said the Father, at last.

Not bad. That was a new one. Beulah smiled around her crooked jaw, giddy as only a new convert could be.

They wrapped her hand and her chest in bandages and sent her back to work. For the next few days every time Beulah looked up at that scaffolding, she could see the bloody streak from where her hand caught. If she looked down, she could see the little spatter where she fell. Her ribs hurt, and would hurt for days and days, but she didn't much mind.

The throbbing faded, but the voice of the Machine didn't.

Beulah limped home. Her ribs ached something fierce. Her hand was bandaged thick, but her head was full of echoes.

"Oh, there you are," said Ma, without looking at her. "Pa's got an interview tomorrow. Help me dredge some water to throw on him, y'hear?"

Ever since her fall, Father Calhoun and Mama Rose seemed just a bit more approving of Beulah. The other girls still volunteered her for the tough work, the dangerous work, but she got an extra pat on the shoulder or an extra sip of water.

"Beulah, you got lunch?" asked Mama Rose.

She waited for Beulah to shake her head. Her brothers had brought some canned fish home from their paper routes, but it'd been an odd color and twitched liberally. The boys had eaten it all before she'd gotten to put any aside for the day.

Mama Rose sawed her own sandwich in half.

"Here," she said. "You'll need to build some muscle up there."

If Beulah ate, it was in the scaffolds. The other girls fell over themselves to avoid doing checks up there, but Beulah found it blessedly peaceful. The workmen didn't ask questions as she tiptoed between them, and she liked the topside view of the Machine as it looked more and more like something whole.

But sometimes her body reminded her she was yet on the mortal plane, an audible twist in her gut that gave even the workmen pause.

"It talks more than you," one of them said. That was Beulah's cue to squeeze herself up onto a bar and tend to her grumbling stomach.

She leaned her cheek against the metal as she ate. She closed her eyes—she could feel the banging of the hammers. She could feel the voice of the Machine.

Hey, hey, hey. Sing for me. Sing.

The Machine never demanded tribute, but the workmen gave it. Blood and sweat aplenty rested on the altar of its workbenches.

One morning the docks were quiet. Beulah learned from the whispers of the other girls what had happened. One of the night shift workers offered his body in full. He'd been up in the scaffolds, installing a bar. He'd taken a bad step. He'd taken another bad step to correct it. He commended himself to the engine room below. He'd gone limp, like you were supposed to, but he'd just been too far out, and a hit a few bars on the way down.

He fell silent as an angel, so it was the morning shift who found him, arms spread and empty eyes staring up at the sky through the half-finished hull. The company put up tarps and ferried his body out as quick as can be. His name was Marco. That was the beginning and end of what any of the girls knew about him.

"Enough, all of you," grumbled Calhoun. "He hasn't left."

He added, under his breath, "Lucky bastard."

The next morning, they reopened the engine block. The workmen touched the doorframe in the same spot as they filed in. Solemn and envious, every one of them.

Staring at the dark stain on the engine room floor, Beulah knew that'd nearly been her.

Hey, hey, sing me a song.

Beulah wasn't good at talking. Ma didn't like the sound of her broken voice, so she didn't get much practice at it, but Beulah learned listening years ago.

Hey, hey, are you there?

She listened to Gran and her list of bodily complaints. She'd listened to her brothers, always fighting in the back of the jalopy. She'd listened to the Cousins Darling, how they picked on everyone and everything. They weren't looking for answers, and surely not from their dumb cousin with the thick tongue.

Hey, hey, sing something for me.

But the Machine wasn't looking for a listener. The men listened plenty. They listened in shifts, all night, as they banged away at its rising hull.

Sing a song or something.

It liked songs, but Beulah wasn't much good for those. She could only hum along with the workmen's hymns, and nothing that could carry through the work floor's smoke. The Machine had those aplenty.

Sing, sing, sing.

Gran.

Gran. Gran worked on the farm. They all worked on the farm. She did, her Pa did, Beulah's Pa did. It was like her feet were rooted in the soil. When she got too old to work, she planted herself on the porch. She stitched and bitched with the best of 'em.

Beulah didn't want the Machine to tell anyone she knew how to stitch and bitch. Only Gran was allowed the privilege.

Gran swore at just about everyone, except Beulah. She liked Beulah because she didn't talk too much. She liked her because she didn't fidget. She liked her because she held out her hands and let her wind the yarn around them when she was rolling it into those balls. She would then set them around her bench while she worked on her latest quilt.

"We're women of the earth," she used to say. Gran's face was brown and wrinkled from the sun, so Beulah believed her. "You and me, Beulah, we got to keep it together. These shits sure can't."

Didn't have much to say to that, but for Gran, that was just fine.

But the soil went bad. The skies went dry. It seemed every day more and more people were leaving. The farm changed owners. The owners left the state. Uncle Darling was the first of the Wanes collective to leave. After a while he sent word of work in San Joaquin Valley. War's bringing something in, finally.

Pa decided it was as good a time as any to start packing. Once the jalopy was loaded up with everything it could carry, he walked up to the porch, all tensed for a fight.

"Ma," he said. "We're leaving tomorrow."

"Like hell I am," said Gran, hissing like a cat.

"Ma," he said. "There hasn't been anything here for years now."

"There's our roots," said Gran. She banged her bare foot on the boards, just to make the point.

Pa sighed. This was back before he drank, so he sighed a lot. "We'll grow somewhere else."

"I won't."

"I'll pick you up and carry you," said Pa.

"I'll drop dead first," said Gran.

Pa rubbed his head and went back to tying down packs to the roof of the car. Gran looked at Beulah out of the corner of her eye. Pa hadn't noticed her there at all.

"I'll show him," she said, with a wicked grin. "You watch, Beulah. You be a rock, just like me."

Then she shut her eyes. Beulah sat with her well into the night. The next morning Pa came out to find her stiff on her bench, her last quilt wrapped over her lap, and her now grey hands clutching her needles. She'd stopped breathing somewhere around midnight.

"Oh, Ma. For Christ's sake," was all Pa said. They buried her out back. Beulah took her sewing tin. She used it to store what little she owned.

Beulah learned an important lesson from Gran—how you became a rock.

The Machine wasn't a rock, though its bones had probably been dug from them a long, long time ago. The more Beulah worked, the harder her skin got. Soon she stopped feeling it when the sparks rained down from above, as the men brought their worship into the upper decks.

Her skin rang like a metal sheet. Ma winced when she slapped her.

"Stop speaking nonsense," said Ma, rubbing her hand. "This happened 'cause of you!"

One of the cousins had gone missing in the piles. He'd seen a pair of shoes dangling on the top. Beulah tried to warn him not to go, tried to warn him the junk had its own mind and its own reasons. The cousins never had the patience to listen to her.

"Whatever, she's just an idiot." He tried to shove her when she reached out to stop them, but she was heavier than she used to be. She just stood and stared, unphased. He tried to hit her with the bat he'd picked up from the edge of the pile, but it just bent on her shoulder.

"What the hell," he said, dropping it like it burned. He backed away. "What the hell?"

Beulah dropped her hand.

"A'ight," she said. She let him go.

There wasn't even a sound when the pile closed. The shoes were still swaying when the rest of the collective found Beulah, still staring at it.

That night, when Ma tried to hit her again, Beulah caught her hand.

"Don't," she said. "It'll hurt."

Beulah didn't mean herself. Ma's eyes went wild like a captured animal. Beulah wasn't holding her hard, but she couldn't pull away. When Beulah uncurled her hand and let her go, she thought she heard her bones squeal like a hinge.

Calhoun had a radio he played on the work floor. At first, it said things like how the War was going, how to buy bonds to protect the troops. My fellow Americans. My friends. My patriots. My faithful.

Over time the president's voice became a deep bassy hum. Over time the ads became choirs. You, yes, you, you're going to save the world. *You, yes you. Tell me who you are. Please, please, please. Give me more than just your blood.*

San Jose had no work. Palo Alto chased them out. Fresno never let them in. The jalopy they'd piled up with all their earthly belongings died in a ditch off the 101. They shoved the poor old girl into the lot of a dusty rest station. Pa dug a few pennies out from between the seats to buy Beulah's younger brothers an apple turnover to split from the diner and the rest of them some hot water. The rest of them squeezed the ketchup packets and salt into their cups. They squeezed onto the sun-flaked bench outside, while Pa asked about repairs at the garage next door.

The owner asked where they were headed. Pa told them.

"San Joaquin?" The mechanic smacked his knee, a layer of grit flew up when he did. "On that junkheap? You'll be lucky if you make it ten miles more. Now, I can get you those last ten miles, but you're better off selling her to me for parts and walk the rest of the way. You'd have a better shot of getting there."

"How much?"

The mechanic told him. It was a total grift.

"What's the nearest town?"

"That'd be San Cicaro," said the mechanic, the smug smile faded. "But you ain't gonna want to go there."

His eyes traveled nervously up the road, where the air was hazy with heat as noon set in. Beulah thought she saw at least three tall figures standing a ways off, watching them. One of them pointed, urgently.

"Mama," asked Beulah. "Who are those people over there?"

"Don't make your idiot noises now, Beulah," said her mother, distracted trying to figure out the fairest way to split the turnover between three hungry boys. "Pa's talking business."

They didn't sell the jalopy. Pa and the Collective Cousins patched it up best they could on their own. They pushed on, following the exits to San Cicaro. Beulah kept an eye out for those folks watching from the side of the road, but they'd faded under the press of the midday heat.

When Beulah cut her leg on a nail that hadn't been fully hammered down, the blood that welled up under her hand came through black.

More. It banged between her ears like the hammer that should've gotten it. *More, more, more.*

Leila Tac was a Mission Indian. She and her brother Tom had run away from the reservation. They'd hopped a barb wire fence to leave. They'd hoped to find work but they found San Cicaro instead.

Beulah ate with them, when she still could, whenever her brothers took her share of the stewpot. It happened more and more. The Machine's services grew longer and longer.

"Your fault for coming in late," said Ma, before she stopped looking at her.

Beulah had met Leila while digging for tubers under one of the wrecked cars. She waved Beulah over. "My brother brought home scrap meat from work. Might as well make sure it all gets eaten, yeah?"

Beulah had helped them fix the roof on their hovel. By now, she was a good climber, and knew something about turning metal into bone. It was the least she could do to give thanks.

Tom worked for a meat packer and Leila sewed military uniforms. Folks in the shanty town avoided them.

"People like that, they said, they'll tap into the bones of San Cicaro itself. They worship the land, you know? Only thing I'm worshipping is whatever I can send my mom," said Leila. "They're killing us out there, you know? Probably hoping we'll die and save them the trouble. At least San Cicaro is San Cicaro. I sure didn't make it that way."

"Is it wicked?" asked Beulah.

Leila had to squint to understand her, but she was patient about it.

"It's just what it is," she said. "Where'd you find work, anyway?"

"Docks," said Beulah. "Working the Machine."

"Oh," said Leila. She looked Beulah up and down, as if trying to decide if Beulah a preacher or something stranger. She fiddled with her saucepan, but in the end, she let her stay. Then, "Explains your tracks."

Leila pointed out the door. Beulah looked down. Puddles gathered outside. It had been raining the last few days. Beulah loved the rain. There'd been so little of it back on the farm near the end. While it rained, Ma went out to find wherever Pa had wandered off to and everyone struggled to bring the laundry in. Beulah had kicked off her ratty boots and walked back and forth through the junkyard, watching the purple clouds gather overhead.

When Beulah looked at the ground, she saw deep grooves in the mud like a truck had been through, but she hadn't heard anything like that for days.

Something was wrong with the engine room. The high priests of the Machine gathered. The foreman bitched and growled. The engineers scratched their head.

"Maybe Marco—"

"Don't be an idiot," said Father Calhoun. "He's still here."

That put a hush on the factory floor. No amount of banging or squealing could seem to get the power running. They sent Beulah to examine the connections. She crawled all through the wiring. It felt slippery and alive. She couldn't tell if the heartbeat she heard came from inside her ears or out.

But there was nothing out of place. This caused more mutterings.

"Going to need a little more, I guess," said Father Calhoun.

It was Mama Rose who stepped forward, cracking what was left of her knuckles, "I'll see what we can do."

Later that day, the engineers all let out a whoop. Praise the lord! Praise the Machine! The power ran through the engine room just fine. Father Calhoun said a prayer and rapped the door. Mama Rose asked Beulah if she'd like to take an extra shift that night. One of the other girls missed her shift the night before. They'd need a few extra hands.

Ma kicked the jalopy that morning. Beulah jumped awake. "Where were you? Why didn't you stop him?"

She didn't wait for an answer, Aunt Darling was sobbing back around the front of the shack.

They lost a second Cousin Darling to the junkpile. He thought he'd heard his brother calling for a hand, he'd told a neighbor before he left. Everyone in the town heard when the pile crashed down on him, but no one dared to leave their shacks to check.

The flanks of the Machine got higher. The cranes came in, lifting materials from one level to the next. The scaffolds held the ribs in place. The girls were sent higher and higher. None climbed higher than Beulah. Sometimes, she'd spent half a day simply crawling through the backside of a reinforced wall. She wasn't always sure she'd come out again.

The higher and farther she climbed, the more clearly she could hear it as the fans began to gasp. The breath of the Machine. The walls under her palms were warm. She could feel the grooves of the wires, like veins in the crook of a wrist.

Pa put on a clean shirt. Ma cut up her last nightgown to make a tie for him. Pa visited all the shops and warehouses on the list. Pa found work right away in San Cicaro.

They needed someone to dredge a lake. They needed the metal for the War. Okie or Arkie didn't matter. If you had strong arms, were willing to work long hours, and didn't talk to any of those union men, you'd do just fine, they said.

The first night, Pa came back beaming.

"We're doing good work there," he said. "They found something under the water. Something big. We'll be getting bonds for it. Even you'll stay fed, Beulah."

Beulah liked having a full stomach, back then.

The second night Pa came back soaking wet. His smile was a little shaky. "I'm all right, Pauleen. Don't fuss. It's just been a busy night."

Ma tried to wipe the mud from his face, but he stayed up the rest of the night, eyes on the door.

The third night Pa came back covered in a black substance that was too oily to be mud, but too sticky to be oil. He didn't say anything. He didn't come in to say good evening, just sat out by the firepit. When Ma and Beulah finally noticed him, he jumped back like their eyes burned him. He pulled off all his clothes. Ma managed to herd him into the shack.

"What happened?" she asked. Pa just shook his head. She got him into his cot, but a few hours later Beulah found him out front again, starkers and staring straight up at the night sky like it was out to get him.

"Ma wants you to wear clothes," said Beulah.

For once and only once, he looked right at her like he understood.

"Forget 'em," he said. "Burn 'em."

When Ma washed his work shirt later, the black stuff squirmed away from the water right off, but the dark brown-red stains of blood ran all the way up to the elbows. She wadded it up and chucked it at one of the junk piles. Beulah fished it out and did what Pa asked. It sparked blue and green when she did it, but the embers floated up into the sky. She could breathe a little easier after that.

That was how you made ash.

Pa didn't do a lot of work after that. Pa didn't do a lot of anything after that. He never said what happened, and when Ma tried to go to the lake to collect pay for the work he did finish, she found the equipment had been dragged away. No one could say there'd ever been a dredging at all.

They got the Darling boy back from the piles. There was only one of him now, but his arms were now two different lengths, and his eyes two different colors. He wore nice clean new loafers. The pair that'd been dangling off the top of the pile.

"Hey, Ma," he said, beaming. He had a mole under his eye like one brother, and a dimple on his chin like the other. "Told you we'd get 'em."

Word spread around the shanty town. The piles, folks muttered, they give things back. People started going missing, one after the other. Soon all you could hear at night was the crunch of the rubble. Soon during the day, there were a lot more empty spaces in the morning sermons. The piles got higher. The piles blocked the morning sun.

One afternoon Beulah backed out of an incomplete corridor to find Marco standing at the end of the hall.

"Hullo," she said, because Gran had taught her to be polite, even if Gran had no patience for it herself. "You all right there?"

Marco stared at her with his big oil-black eyes.

"Sure am," he said, after a bit. "Got a sandwich under there?"

He nodded at the bulge under her patchy coveralls. Beulah pulled it out and held it out.

"Mostly tomatoes," she said. "Not sure what kind."

Tom and Leila had tried growing vegetables against the wall of their shack. They'd wriggled alarmingly, but they were edible. They made Beulah take some every morning, even if Beulah said she wasn't much hungry anymore.

Marco took a bite. He only had a few teeth left. The crumbs fell at his feet, on a sticky patch of floor where his shadow should have been. She wasn't sure what kind of offering that counted for but from the shifting of the plates above, she supposed it'd do.

"Hm," he said. "Tastes alive. You're out by the Old Transfer Station, right?"

"Sure am," said Beulah. "But how'd you know that?"

"Cause you told me," said Marco, grinning. He nodded upwards, that knowing, smug kind of nod you got when a priest talked about the man upstairs. "Us, anyway. We like it when you talk."

It was such a strange thing to hear. Beulah laughed. She wasn't sure she'd ever done that before. It sounded a little like a cough. "That's new."

"So are we." Marco winked, with his one bloodshot eye. "Am I bothering you?"

"Nah," said Beulah. "Been here longer than me, haven't you?"

"I'm a lifer," he said. "Take it, by the way."

"What?"

But Marco had his own shift to cover. He shoved his hands back into his bloodied overalls and strolled down the hall. An hour later, Mama Rose came by to tell her they needed an extra to cover the five-to-twelve. Beulah said sure.

It seemed the sort of advice you ought to take.

The fires were still burning by the time she came home that night. The trucks were lined up like a barricade. The logos were big with white eyes blazing along the side. They wanted people to see them. They wanted people to be afraid. Women and children screaming as men with gun belts dragged them into the trucks in twos and threes.

A man in a vest touched Beulah's arm. He nudged her and nudged her. It was only after her work shirt tore at the shoulder that she realized he'd been trying to pull her. She looked up at him.

"Got someplace else to be," she said. "Sorry."

The man swore and tried to punch her. She didn't bother to warn him like she'd warned Ma. He must've broken his hand on her jaw, because he swore something fierce and let her go.

"Bye now," said Beulah. She turned and walked away, towards the piles. Thunder crashed. Something brushed the back of her head, blowing her hair forward. She reached back. Her fingers brushed the hot bullet wedged against the back of her neck, squashed flat like a coin.

"Huh," she said. Because it looked so much like candy, and she hadn't had candy in a good long while, she tucked it under her tongue and swallowed it. It burned hot going down. It was a nice, spicy feel.

The man stopped bothering her after that.

The shanty town was in shambles. People running, and screaming. They either ran into the detectives or ran into the piles, both were equally happy to have them. Beulah thought she spotted what was left of the Collective Cousins sitting cross-legged on an old ice box, singing some old commercial jingle, but she didn't stop to check.

A few more bullets tickled her cheek and shoulders, tearing a hole or two in her coveralls. She made a note to mend those when she got the chance. Eventually she stopped feeling it. The gas got thick enough their aim got bad. A looter tried to knock her over. She held out her arm and let him run into it. He fell back and didn't move. Beulah stepped through one of the burning shacks. No one followed her.

The rain came and shut everyone up.

The fires were down to a low smolder by the time Beulah reached the family shack. The jalopy was on its side. The north end of the shack was bent inwards, as if struck by a great force from above. The fire pot and the clothesline were gone, along with all the clothes and the cookware. There were tracks leading to the piles and tracks leading to the trucks. Beulah wasn't sure which belonged to Ma and her brothers. She found Pa sleeping against the jalopy. There wouldn't be any waking him anymore. He looked pretty relieved, all told.

"Beulah?"

Beulah turned her head. Her charred clothes hung off her in tatters. Her hair crackled as the rain hit it. Leila backed away on instinct, but Beulah held up her hand to dampen the glare from her eyes, and Leila relaxed a little.

"Oh," she said. "It *is* you. I'm so sorry—your mother, she took the boys and ran out into the piles… I tried to warn them, but…"

"Tom?" asked Beulah. Leila's face fell.

"I don't know, I don't know. The union boys were calling everyone in. He went… he went somewhere. Idiot," she admitted. She took Beulah's hand, and gave it a few tugs. "Look, there's a drainage ditch that-away, we can hide out there and figure out who's left. I might know someone north. We can find work. We can find the others. We can…"

Beulah turned away and knelt next to the ruined hood of the jalopy. She nudged her Pa aside to wrench the hood off. It went with a whining screech. Leila covered her mouth. Beulah pulled out Gran's sewing tin. She pushed them into Leila's arms.

"Think it's about three month's pay," said Beulah. "Should be good for something. If my Ma don't want it, yours sure will."

"What?" It took Leila a minute or two to process. She was awfully distracted, so Beulah took her hands and folded them over the tin, to make sure she didn't drop them.

"Don't need it," said Beulah. "I'm going to be a rock."

She turned and walked back the way she came, past the collapsed shacks and the receding piles, pulling back like the tides. A few women and children picked their way over the remnants. Someone was crying. Someone was praying. It didn't sound like the prayers Beulah knew anymore.

Beulah walked back to the docks. The soles of her boots had melted away ages ago, but that was fine. Her feet thickened ages ago. They left scorched tracks in her wake. The guards in front of the shipyard had guns. Fancy assault weapons. Best that the government could buy them.

"Ma'am, could we convince you not to?" the soldier asked, very carefully.

"Sir, I work here," said Beulah.

He backed away. Beulah nodded and moved on.

The night worshippers were in, clanking away. The Machine was never completely at rest. Machines never were, but she felt the floor go from hard to soft as stepped into its mighty hull. There was Father Calhoun, changing the piece on his drill. There was Mama Rose, passing out water. There was Marco, on the scaffolding.

"Clear the floor," said Beulah. "It's past time."

Father Calhoun rang the bell.

Beulah wandered the halls of the Machine.

It was empty now. The tarps and workbenches all abandoned. Beulah felt the flooring under her feet go soft and supple, like muscles tensing for something.

Beulah ran her fingertips along the completed panels. At first, they left screeching sparks, but when she pressed her palm down fully, it smoothed out like skin.

Beulah found the engine block. It'd been finished a while ago, ceiling and everything. She settled herself against the engine, listening to it beat. *Missed you, missed you.*

It'd hoped she'd come back. Beulah smiled so hard it hurt. Her face wasn't really built for it anymore.

"Don't care about the War," she said, as the wires folded over her. They slid under her paneling, clicking into place. "Want to go someplace else?"

And, pulsing in agreement, the Machine began to move.

It tore out its moorings. It tore out the cradle. The scaffolding shivered and splintered like toothpicks, as its mighty sides heaved. The ramp went slick, with oil, with blood, it was hard to say, but the Machine's incomplete bow split open like a mouth. And through those jagged steel teeth, it laughed as it shoved itself backwards into the waiting sea.

The morning radio programs would have their own songs to sing.

"*Accident in dry dock. Critical design flaws. Weak moorings. A complete structural collapse. The chains had buckled, the ropes had snapped, and the entire ship had pitched half-finished down the ramp and into the waves.*

Investigation pending. Shipments to be redirected."

The workmen stood in scattered confusion in the shipyard, watching as the jagged shadow cut its way through the dark grey water, sharp against the searchlights as it made for the open water. Father Calhoun began to bang his wrench against what was left of the dock. Mother Rose began to hum. One by one, they threw up their arms and fell to their knees.

Glory, Hallelujah. The work was done. Amen.

Headline Space for Mysteries

Olivia was stunned.

There was little to go on. The newspaper detailed an accident at the docks, sure. Some chains broke and the entire mooring came undone. The USS *Fairweather* had slipped into the water and vanished.

Following details were sparse. Shipments were rerouted to San Francisco and San Diego for fear of freighters being damaged by the underwater wreckage. The *San Cicaro Observer* took comments from supervisors about the mud being too deep, but such statements didn't make sense. Not when other ships had been using that channel for some time.

More perplexingly... the wreckage had never been found.

Olivia looked through the next day's newspaper. Then the day that followed. There was nothing. She suspected that the Office of Censorship had put the kibosh on any more stories about the debacle for the sake of the war. Morale considerations or some such excuse. But to have the event excised so completely from all records? That was very strange.

There were other articles that mentioned "the accident," but they were more about the state of San Cicaro's economy as a whole. Like how the shipyard's production was placed on hiatus pending internal audits. This was just before the war ended, and the Strike Wave of 1945 swept across the United States. If the investigators found anything, their announcement was lost in the deluge of labor troubles and runaway inflation.

I guess there's only ever so much headline space for mysteries, Olivia thought, sighing. Glancing at her to do list, she reminded herself that this dalliance was not part of her assignment. She could always come back to this later, and maybe pitch an article of her own on the subject.

Checking the clock, it was not *quite* lunch time yet, so she got up and sought the next few editions on her list.

She grinned when she recognized the image that popped up on the next newspaper on the screen. It was of a Ferris Wheel, behind a sign that read "Demitri's Garden of Delights." It was about the founding of the amusement park that preceded the wondrous farmer's market where she always got the freshest produce.

Finally, she thought. *A story that doesn't sound depressing.*

Garibaldi Pearls
Ian Ableson

The Californian beach before them was very unlike the South American beaches that Mauricio was used to. The sand was greyer, the water was darker, and the sun didn't shine quite as brightly. Clumps of half-decayed seaweed competed with cigarette butts for space in the sand. The people were different too. It was a beautiful summer day, and hardly anyone was enjoying the water. Indeed, he was surprised by the lack of crowds on the beach. Others, such as those on the boardwalk, were supremely overdressed for life by the ocean.

Although he wasn't exactly one to judge at that moment.

Mauricio shifted uncomfortably in his new suit. Despite being in his early thirties, he'd never worn a suit in his life. The lines that already creased his dark, chestnut-colored skin reflected a life of hard work under the incessant gaze of the ever-shining island sun. His coal-black hair and beard had been carefully manicured for this meeting.

Thankfully, his partner was more than happy to handle the brunt of the talking. Mauricio watched as Glenn Reed showed off the equipment to their prospective investor with admirable aplomb.

"And this… metal cylinder…" said Mr. Gray uncertainly.

"Holds the air! Enough for a man to stay underwater for nearly half an hour," Glenn said excitedly, his forefinger pinched to his thumb as he spoke. Mauricio's partner was also in his early thirties, but his clean-shaven face, shock of orange-red hair, and natural exuberance gave him the appearance of a much younger man. His tan pinstripe suit was perhaps five or six years out of fashion and a little worn at the knees and the elbows.

It was the suit of a man who either had little money to spare on fashion or was so easily distracted that he failed to notice modern trends. Mauricio smiled slightly. In the case of Glenn Reed, it might have been both.

Stanley Gray, Entertainment Director for San Cicaro Boardwalk Entertainment, rapped his knuckles skeptically against the tank. He stroked his greying moustache as he considered the device.

"Like Jacques Cousteau?" he asked. Mr. Gray himself was in his early sixties, with more hair in his moustache than remained on his scalp, but age had not dulled his wits. If anything, it had sharpened them.

"Like the great explorer himself!" said Glenn grandly. He threw his hands out wide in his excitement, eyes gleaming at the future he envisioned. "Think about it! Why, the newspaper ads practically write themselves. 'Explore the Ocean at San Cicaro's Boardwalk Park!' 'Dive Without a Care in the World!' 'No Reef Out of Reach, No Depth too Deep for the Underwater Experience of a Lifetime!'"

Mauricio cleared his throat meaningfully. He arched an eyebrow at Glenn, who lost a little steam at the interruption.

"Ah… Yes…" Glenn recovered with a smile. "Harmless exaggeration, I assure you, just to get folks excited. My partner here has informed me that there *are* depths too deep to dive safely, especially for the untrained. But we wouldn't be taking our visitors down that deep, no sir. Get most folks twenty feet down so they can look an eel in the eye as they'll be pleased as punch."

"Hmm…" Mr. Gray hummed noncommittally. He held up one of the two floppy tubes connected to the tank and peered quizzically into it. "And you said it was called… Scooda?"

"S.C.U.B.A. Diving. It stands for Self-Contained Underwater Breathing Apparatus," said Glenn with pride. "I tell you, if San Cicaro Boardwalk Entertainment jumps at this opportunity now, you won't regret it! This technology is so new that even marine scientists have barely started using it. Why, I'll bet you that the tank you see before you and the three back at our hotel room are the only ones of their like for five hundred miles in every direction. If you'll loan my partner and I a small sum to cover our starting costs—let's say a thousand dollars or so—we'll be able to set up a little shop next to your boardwalk, selling the greatest grand tours of ocean! Once word gets out, you'll have to beat the crowds off with a stick!"

Mr. Gray gingerly handed the tube back to Glenn. "Well, Mr. Reed, I can see you're enthusiastic. But maintaining the popularity of an entertainment complex as large and," Stanley Gray paused for a moment, casting his eyes skyward as he searched for the right word, "*varied* as the San Cicaro Boardwalk Park requires that we be very selective with our attractions. Trusting in new technology like this isn't usually our way of business. How can I be sure that your scuba diving won't just prove to be some crazy fad like those madmen who used to sit on top of flagpoles? And what if something went wrong with the equipment?"

Glenn Reed didn't look discouraged. If anything, his smile grew wider. He clapped a hand on Mauricio's shoulder. "What you need, Mr. Gray, is a demonstration! A little proof that we—and all of this crazy equipment—are worth your investment! My partner here, Mauricio Zambrano, came all the way from a tiny little speck of land off the coast of Venezuela called the *Isla Margarita* to join me in this business venture. Now, on Margarita Island Mr. Zambrano is known as one of the best pearl divers to ever shuck an oyster. In San Cicaro he'll be known as the best undersea guide a man could ever want. How long would you say you can hold your breath, Mauricio?"

"Eight minutes," said Mauricio, his neutral tone a far cry from his partner's enthusiasm.

Glenn whooped. "Eight minutes! I'll bet you and I could only handle two or three tops, eh Mr. Gray? So here's what we're gonna do. I'll put on all this scuba gear. Then my partner and I will both take a little afternoon dip in the ocean, me with the equipment and him with nothing but his lungs. I guarantee you that he'll break the surface long before you see hide or hair of me! What do you say?"

The smallest hint of a smile played on Gray's lips. "Very well. A demonstration. When you're ready, Mr. Reed."

Glenn practically vibrated with excitement. If it weren't for the awkward bundle of scuba diving equipment in his arms, Mauricio thought he might have danced a jig on the spot. "Neptune's domain shall soon be ours to explore! Mauricio, will you find us the rocks while I don the tank?"

Mauricio nodded, but Mr. Gray's brow furrowed. "Rocks? What do you need rocks for?"

"To sink," said Mauricio frankly. "The human body floats without additional weight. Holding onto large stones is the easiest way to stay at depth for long periods of time. Mr. Reed says that the man who gave him the tanks is designing suits with weights on them that will solve the issue. But until such technology is available, we use rocks."

"Marvelous," said Gray. "Progress never ceases."

He spoke to Glenn for a few moments about mundane matters—intended price of admission, marketing strategies, open hours—while Mauricio scoured the beach for stones of the appropriate size. He returned with two rocks of around seven or eight pounds. Not huge, but enough to overcome their bodies' natural buoyancies and sink them into the sea.

Mauricio suppressed a smile when he returned to find Glenn stripped of his pinstripes, revealing a pair of swim trunks as out-of-touch as the suit itself. He kept his undershirt on however, lest he complain later of the harness' horrible chafing. He slipped the compressed air tank over his shoulders, letting the regulator mouthpiece dangle from a hose. His fins forced him to shuffle around awkwardly, flapping spatulas that slapped the sand with every step. And to top it all off, there was the mask—a slapdash, homemade, and ill-fitting oval of plastic strapped to Glenn's face like the bottom of a goldfish bowl.

Mauricio knew that Glenn didn't truly understand the engineering behind the gas compression, or the regulator, or the pressure valves. Yet he'd practiced with the gear often enough to have a practical knowledge of how to use it without inhaling a lung full of seawater. Mauricio worried about what they would do if the equipment ever broke down, but Glenn was confident they would have money to hire specialists long before then.

Amazing, Mauricio thought as Glenn tightened the straps around his body. *All of this just to let a man survive a little longer in an environment that wasn't meant for him. We'll be scuba diving straight to the moon next.*

"Mauricio! We're up, partner!" Glenn called. "You just wait and see, Mr. Gray. Mauricio will be back up in eight or nine minutes, and I'll stay down at least double that amount!"

"I look forward to it," said Mr. Gray, and he settled himself on an outcropping of rock to watch.

The moment Mauricio's toes were below the water, he was struck by a wave of serenity. The Pacific might be colder and grayer than the sunny seas of Isla Margarita, but it was still the sea. If Mauricio were a whale, he would swim south, following the Chilean coast to Tierra del Fuego, then hug South America's eastern coastline until he was back in his Venezuela. Something about this new city filled Mauricio with a perpetual sense of unease, but the sense of connectedness with his homeland calmed him.

An exclamation to Mauricio's right broke him out of his reverie as Glenn stumbled and nearly fell. The American had to walk backwards into the sea to avoid tripping over the fins, leaving him vulnerable to every unexpected stone. Glenn waved off Mauricio's steadying hand, taking the awkward steps one at a time like a newborn lamb. Eventually he managed to stumble far enough into the depths that the water lapped at his chest. With an encouraging thumbs up to Mauricio, Glenn popped the regulator into his mouth and sank beneath the waves. Mauricio pulled down his own pair of goggles—preferring the clarity of vision they provided compared to a full mask—and slipped into the sea.

Given their proximity to shipping lanes and expanding industrial centers, the waters of San Cicaro should not have been nearly as clear as they were. He could see a marvelous distance. In the shallows, there was only sand and stone and a lone porcupinefish which, though initially startled, now seemed content to ignore him entirely. But further out to sea, the ocean floor made a gentle descent until it reached a depth of perhaps twenty or twenty-five feet. Even from here, Mauricio could see that the waters at that depth were teeming with life.

Mauricio glanced at Glenn to see if his partner was equally taken with the marine display before them. Glenn however, paid no attention to the deeper waters, or anything else around them for that matter. He sat on the ocean floor perhaps a foot below the surface clutching his rock, eyes tightly shut behind the mask. He breathed rapidly, teetering on the edge of hyperventilation. Had they been on land, Mauricio would have sighed in exasperation. He looked at the rock in his own hands. He really should be concentrating on conserving energy if he was to stay below for the promised eight minutes.

Then again, once their business was established he would be expected to lead groups of tourists through these waters, wouldn't he? He looked back to the deeper waters, understanding he would need to learn them sooner or later. Besides, it only really mattered how long Glenn stayed underwater for their demonstration.

Mauricio dropped his weight stone and swam towards the undersea mecca.

Large, eroded rocks provided a foundation around which all the other living creatures had consolidated. The rocks gave the bottom of the ocean an unexpectedly municipal feel. They were the buildings, the bridges, and the tunnels, and all of the creatures of the sea lived their busy lives intertwined amongst them. Mauricio took careful hold of a boulder to maintain his depth as he surveyed the area, ignoring the slimy feel of algae below his fingers. It might be wise to get gloves for their clients. Spiny gray-blue sea urchins dotted the rocks like thistle flowers, slowly making their inevitable way around the structures as they consumed the algae. Rippling towers of kelp between the stones reached high enough to caress the ocean surface, little silver fish darting erratically around them. Discarded shells from all matter of mollusks littered the ocean floor. A crab swiftly buried itself into the sand, trying to avoid Mauricio's piercing gaze among the tiny bits of algae and sand.

Although many of the fish were strange to him, Mauricio was able to pick out a few species from the guides he'd been studying. A lone California sheephead swam by, a bizarrely colored fish with a single wide maroon stripe bisecting the darker coloration at the head and tail. He spotted striped bass and rockfish. There were garibaldi, the foot-long orange fish that protected their territories without an ounce of fear. To Mauricio's amazement, he even spotted a sea lion watching him, but it arced gracefully away the moment he looked at it.

Any fears that Mauricio had about the feasibility of entertaining tourists within Californian waters swiftly vanished.

Mauricio pushed off the rock and continued exploring the seascape. He pinballed from stone to stone as he swam to maintain his speed, taking note of the best handholds to anchor himself and others.

Out of the corner of his eye he saw a flash of purple, and his heart skipped a beat. Coral! He didn't think there was any coral in this part of California. He quickly abandoned his handhold and made a beeline to it.

It was so similar to the coral of Venezuela—the stony appearance, the vibrant purple, the stubborn resistance to the currents—that he had to smile. The only difference was how it grew. Rather than covering the rocks, this species appeared to grow straight out of the sand, like some technicolor shrub. Mauricio could see perhaps a dozen such corals, each nearly as tall as he was, scattered across the ocean floor.

As he drew closer to them, something gave Mauricio pause. Each coral appeared to be growing out of a raised mound of sand. For a moment, he had an impression of shapes within the mounds. The body of a seal, the tail of a whale, the unmistakable fins of a ray, innumerable smaller fish. And out of the very corner of his vision… a shape like a human leg. Mauricio blinked, and the mounds of sand were nothing more than mounds.

Something glinted in the sand between the corals, something that was neither stone nor shell. Mauricio reached into the sand and pulled out a small orange pearl. He stared in astonishment. It was undoubtedly a pearl—the same luster, same weight, same sheen, same feel between his fingers that he'd known since he could walk. Yet it was colored a brilliant orange, nearly the exact same shade as the garibaldi he'd seen earlier. Even more extraordinarily, there were no oysters in sight—the pearl had simply been lying loose in the sand. With just a casual glance, Mauricio could see a dozen more such pearls within arm's reach. He darted excitedly across the sea floor, plucking pearls from the seabed at every opportunity, although he was careful not to touch the delicate corals despite his excitement.

How was this not known? An entire pearl fishery, twenty-five below sea level near a major urban center? How were there not dozens of divers competing with Mauricio for this spot? And that color! He'd never seen it in a pearl before. In minutes Mauricio held two fistfuls of garibaldi-colored pearls, and plenty more littered the seabed between the mounds of sand. He grinned widely in excitement.

Then the mound nearest to Mauricio shifted. Sand and stone fell away. Bone stuck out of the sand. Curious, Mauricio swam closer. With both of his hands occupied by the pearls, he used his foot to loosen the protruding bone from the mound.

A human pelvis tumbled gently to the sea floor.

Cold terror swept through Mauricio. A vision passed before his eyes, of his quick impression of the shapes of different creatures in the mounds. For a moment he was paralyzed, and then deep-seated survival instincts kicked in. He frantically kicked off the sea floor shooting up towards the surface.

Mauricio had never risen to the surface faster in his life, and he broke the surface of the water like a breaching porpoise. He could hear Mr. Gray laughing from a distance.

"Well, that wasn't even close to eight minutes! Are our Californian waters that cold, Mr. Zambrano?"

Shaking, Mauricio swam fast for the beach, clutching the pearls in his hands so hard that it hurt. For the first time he could remember, Mauricio felt a desperate need to get out of the water. By the time he reached the sand he'd calmed enough to smile at Mr. Gray, feigning composure that he did not feel.

"My apologies. I became distracted exploring the ocean and did not notice I was nearly out of breath. Shall we wait for my partner together?"

Twenty-five minutes later Mauricio still sat in the sand, hiding the pearls in his clenched fists. He was beginning to worry about Glenn. He should have surfaced by now. He turned to Mr. Gray, intending to strike up a conversation to distract himself, but frowned when he noticed that their business associate was behaving rather strangely. The older man was glancing incessantly over his shoulder, eyes constantly scanning the beach.

"Expecting someone else, Mr. Gray?" Mauricio asked politely.

The older man startled, then chuckled self-depreciatively and shook his head. "No, no. Not at all. Just keeping an eye on my shadow."

Mauricio's brows furrowed. Perhaps this was a Californian colloquialism that he didn't understand. "Ah. Is it likely to run away?"

Gray loosed a short barking laugh.

"Run away… hmm, hmm, not exactly. I have lived in San Cicaro for most of my life. To survive in San Cicaro for as many decades as I have, one must give credence to all the stories, however far-fetched they may be." This ominous statement and the underlying tension in Gray's voice meant little to Mauricio, but he nodded politely nonetheless. Thankfully, the man quickly changed the subject. "So, Mr. Zambrano, what is your role in all of this? You mostly kept your peace this morning. At first I thought perhaps you weren't following everything, but your English seems to be excellent."

Mauricio shrugged. "Discussing business propositions is not my area of expertise. Mr. Reed is an American and a businessman, I am neither. I know the ocean—her beauty, her moods, her dangers—but he knows how to pitch an idea."

Gray nodded and made a humming noise in the back of his throat. "And how did you two arrive at this partnership?"

Mauricio reflected for a moment on the series of events that had brought him here. "We met in a town called Porlamar on the Isla Margarita. It's the place where the divers meet with the pearl wholesalers to sell our catch. Mr. Reed came to Venezuela while working as a temporary replacement clerk for one of the New York-based wholesalers. He already had the idea and the scuba equipment—as I understand he bought the tanks off a friend of his who worked on Cousteau's Aqua-Lung—but Mr. Reed is not much of a mariner. He had the idea of using the equipment to introduce the seas to the masses, but in truth he is terrified of deep water."

Gray chortled. "That seems quite the Achilles' Heel for a man wishing to run a diving business."

Mauricio made a noncommittal noise in the back of his throat. "In my experience with him thus far, Mr. Reed has a wonderful head for ideas. However, he has a tendency to get ahead of himself in his excitement. One day while we were negotiating pearl prices, he told me of his aspirations. Together we developed a business plan. I will dive with the customers and show them the wonders of the sea, and he will handle the administrative and financial aspects. It seemed a natural partnership."

Gray stopped walking for a moment and peered piercingly at Mauricio. "And what is the nature of your partnership? What is to be your cut of the take?"

"Assuming we can get the business going, Mr. Reed and I will split everything fifty-fifty. I would not have left my home for less."

Stanley's barking laugh rang out again, and he clapped Mauricio on the shoulder. "Good! That's good. Make sure you keep him to that. I like you, Mr. Zambrano, but then I've always liked the talent more than the business folk, and I can see that you are the talent here. I hire performing troupes for the boardwalk sometimes—acrobats, musicians, parades, and so on—and you would be amazed and disgusted at the number of ways the agents find to cut into a performer's wages. An administrative fee *here*, equipment costs *there*... and before they know it, they're playing horn or slinging each other in the air for pennies on the dollar.

"Especially," he added, his voice suddenly sharper, "especially when the talent is not American. But you mentioned your home, and that brings to mind one last question. You were confident enough in this plan to leave Venezuela? Just like that? A country that I presume has been your home your whole life?"

Mauricio cracked a smile. "Who knows if I'll get another opportunity to see more of the world? Besides, I don't know how many years of diving I have left in me. I am barely past my thirtieth year, but already I see that I am slower than the younger men. This new technology is a wonder to behold. Truth be told, we already make use of diving technology of a sort at the Isla Margarita. We call them scaphander divers. They wear massive helmets that connect them to the boat by a hose, and the men on the boat pump air through the hose into their helmets. They walk along the ocean floor and gather oysters as they find them. But your movement is so restricted in the suits... I prefer to swim freely, even if I have to rely on my own air to do it. With these air tanks, a man could have both the freedom of movement of the free divers and the air supply of the scaphanders."

And if this business venture goes well, Mauricio thought, *I will be able to send money to my sisters and my nephews. The American dollar goes far in Venezuela. If I can make enough in this city so that my family's well-being is no longer dependent on the whims of the harvest and the instability of the pearl market, I will be a happy man.*

Before Mr. Gray could reply, Glenn popped triumphantly out of the ocean. Mauricio sighed with relief at the sight of his partner but said nothing. His concerns could wait. The director laughed and clapped the red-haired man on the shoulder, ignoring the seawater that dripped from him.

"Well, I suppose that proves it well enough for me. And why not? My partners want to add rides to the park, despite my doubts of their prospects. Too many ordinary amusement parks have shut down since the Depression! I need an idea to woo them from their notion, something with… what was that word? The one you used while you were getting ready?"

"Pizzazz!" Glenn shot with a smile. Mauricio's brow rose in surprise. He would have to ask his partner where in the world he discovered these strange, American words. Mr. Gray laughed, clapping his hands together in delight.

"That's the one! Mr. Reed, Mr. Zambrano, I am pleased to inform you that San Cicaro Boardwalk Entertainment is prepared to provide you a starting loan. Although," he stroked his chin thoughtfully, "we may need to negotiate the amount."

Glenn pumped his arm in triumph. "See Mauricio? What'd I tell you? San Cicaro, best city for entrepreneurs and innovators this side of the Rockies! You won't regret this investment, Mr. Gray!"

Mauricio smiled weakly, the pearls digging into his palms.

Despite their win, Mauricio refused any lavish spending in celebration. Thus it took little for Glenn to convince him into a restaurant with a shiny neon sign proclaiming "Missy's Diner" against the encroaching evening. The diner was busy. The sizzle of the fryer competed with the clinking of dishes and silverware to dominate the soundscape. Mauricio was quiet over their dinner of burgers, shakes and fries. Yet Glenn had not noticed, so excited was he in the day's success. His endless stream of words—plans for the future, mostly—was too fast-paced for Mauricio to follow, even if he were calm and focused. Finally, as they were finishing their milkshakes and paying the bill, Mauricio found a chance to get a word in edgewise.

"Glenn," he said abruptly. "I found something in the sea."

Glenn stopped mid-chatter, a final last glob of milkshake on his spoon. "What? Hm? Did you see a dolphin or something? Manta ray? Squid? If it's charismatic enough we'll slap it on the sign, maybe the flyers too!"

Mauricio wordlessly took one of the orange pearls out of his pockets and placed it on the table in front of him. The pearl looked so small and insignificant now, appearing to be nothing more than a solidified speck of sunrise. Glenn picked it up and turned it over in his fingers, his eyes sparkling as he examined it.

"Wow!" he said. "*Wow!* Now that's something! Never heard any talk of pearls in San Cicaro!"

"I have more," said Mauricio quietly, wishing Glenn wouldn't speak so loudly. He didn't want the other diner patrons to overhear.

"More? How many?" Glenn asked, squinting curiously at the pearl between his fingers.

"Maybe two or three dozen in my pockets."

Glenn startled, his eyes widening in surprise. "Two or three dozen? And you got that many in a handful of minutes? How much do you think they're worth?"

"I don't know. If they were white pearls from an oyster then I could guess at a rough estimate, but the color..." Mauricio shook his head. "I can tell you this. With that shape, that luster, that size... every one of them is *de vista*. First quality. To the right collector, they might be worth quite a lot."

The sparkle in Glenn's eyes grew hungrier. He stared at the little pearl as though he could pierce its secrets with the power of his gaze alone. "And... do you think there are more in the same spot?"

"Yes, but..." Mauricio hesitated, choosing his next words carefully. He needed his partner to understand what he was about to say. "I don't think we should be going after those pearls."

Glenn looked his partner in the eye, encouraging Mauricio as he continued.

"The spot where I found them, there's... I'm not sure. I didn't see clearly. But there were these corals growing out of mounds in the sand, and the mounds... I think there were bodies in them, Glenn. Not just animals, either. We can put the sale price of the pearls towards the opening costs, cover anything that Mr. Gray will not. But we must leave that beach alone from here on out. We'll take the tourists somewhere else."

Glenn's eyebrows shot up. "Bodies? Like a graveyard? Well, let's not be so hasty, partner! You know, I grew up in Savannah—that's a town in Georgia, couple thousand miles east of here—and people there used to pay to tour the graveyards all the time. Folks love it! A coral graveyard, now that's even better! Why don't we incorporate it into the tour?"

Mauricio shook his head emphatically. "*Jamás*, Glenn. You weren't there. It's not right. Not safe."

The disappointment was clear in Glenn's face, but he nodded and handed the pearl back to Mauricio. "Whatever you say, partner. You're the one who knows the ocean, after all. We'll work on finding a buyer in the morning. Before we met I used to sell vacuum cleaners door-to-door, selling pearls will be a cinch. We'll talk to Mr. Gray in the morning, shall we? He ought to know some folk."

Mauricio nodded, his shoulders relaxing. No matter how much Glenn talked, Mauricio could count on his partner to listen when it was important.

"Let's go back to the hotel, shall we?" Glenn said with that comfortable smile as he began to shuffle out of the booth. "Lots to do tomorrow. We should get some rest."

"Wow!" Stanley Gray said as he squinted at the pearl between his fingers. "Well, she is a beauty, isn't she? And you have how many of these, Mr. Zambrano?"

"There are 31 more back in the hotel room," answered Mauricio.

"Not bad, not bad at all," Stanley murmured. He placed the pearl back on his desk. "Well, you two were right to come to me. I know a handful of folks who'd love to own such an oddity. Jewelers, entertainers, and if we're lucky maybe even an eccentric millionaire or two. I'll drop a few lines around lunchtime."

"Thank you, sir," said Mauricio.

"My pleasure, my pleasure. Now, assuming someone bites, I'll leave it to the two of you to negotiate. I haven't an inkling what the going rate for orange pearls might be."

"Agreed," said Mauricio, prepared to make up some numbers.

"Now I won't ask you where you got them—not much of a man for the sea myself anyway—but I will ask you if you think there might be more. Any buyer I find that will go for 32 pearls will go for a hundred just as readily."

Mauricio hesitated, glancing at his partner. Glenn remained silent, and in fact had been unusually reticent the entire morning. Presently his gaze was fixed on the window, and he kept fiddling with his right sleeve, seemingly trying to pull it further over his hand.

"No, I think I found them all," said Mauricio after a moment.

"Alright, well, if there aren't any more, then there aren't any more," said Stanley with a smile. "Why don't you both spend the day exploring the city? I'll leave a note with hotel reception if I hear anything."

"Well, sounds like you were right, partner," said Mauricio once they'd stepped outside. "Going to Mr. Gray was just the thing to do."

Glenn said nothing, vacant eyes staring at nothing in particular.

Mauricio felt a lump of concern in his chest. "So, shall we go downtown? Maybe find somewhere for lunch? If we're going to be in this city, we ought to learn its ways."

Glenn still tugged at his sleeve.

"Say, you get an itch or something?" Mauricio touched his partner on the shoulder. "Must be a pharmacy somewhere in this whole mess of buildings."

Glenn released his sleeve and snapped immediately to attention, stepping away from Mauricio's reach a little quickly. "What? No, no, no need for a pharmacy. Sorry partner, I've been a little out of sorts. Didn't sleep well. Tell you what—you take a look downtown and get the lay of the land. I think I'll take a little walk along the beach and clear my head."

Mauricio frowned. "Sure you're alright?"

"Just fine," said Glenn. He gave Mauricio a strained smile. "You've got to learn the ways of an American metropolis. Me? I've got to learn the ways of the ocean if that's how we'll be making our livelihoods. I'll meet you back at the hotel in the evening."

Mauricio watched with consternation as his partner walked away, head in the clouds, ambling vaguely towards the sea.

Stanley Gray worked fast. By the time Mauricio returned to the hotel that evening, there was a message waiting for him at the hotel reception desk.

Divers Extraordinaire,
Found a buyer! Open to price negotiation for oddities. Inflexible in time, not in town for long. Now or never. I am entertaining buyer at my office this evening, please come at your very earliest convenience.
—S.G.

Glenn was not in their shared room. Nor was he in the lobby, the lounge, or the hotel bar. In a moment of suspicion, Mauricio opened the bag that they'd been using to haul around the Scuba equipment. All of the tanks, hoses, masks, and regulators were present and accounted for. After 45 minutes of restless waiting, a frustrated Mauricio left the hotel to expand his search.

He found his partner standing alone on the beach where they'd held the demonstration, staring out into the ocean. Mauricio called to Glenn, but the silhouette didn't move. Something about the sight alarmed Mauricio. Not once, in the time they'd been working together, had he ever seen Glenn stand quite this still.

Mauricio touched Glenn's shoulder, and the man leapt in shock. His eyes swiveled wildly to meet his partner's, and for a moment there was a glint of something alien within them—a deep and desperate yearning, an overpowering desire.

Then the look passed, and Glenn smiled calmly.

"Hey, partner," he said, "What's the rush?"

"How long have you been here? Gray found a buyer, but we've got to get to his office before they leave."

"Hey, that's swell. Swell, isn't it? Just swell. Why don't you go talk with them, partner. You don't need me complicating things." Glenn's gaze slid off Mauricio's face and returned to the ocean as he spoke. His smile never wavered.

"What's gotten into you? This is our chance! We talk this thing out and we could be debt-free in an hour! I might be the man of the ocean, but you're the negotiator. Now come on," Mauricio countered. He grasped Glenn's arm in a tight grip and yanked him to his feet. After a moment's weak resistance, the man followed.

They arrived at Stanley's office to find him entertaining a young woman, seated opposite his desk, each with a glass in front of them.

"There are my scuba boys!" Stanley said with a boisterous laugh. He raised his bourbon in toast. "Gentlemen, I'd like to introduce you to Miss Rosemary Lavoie, a good friend of mine, just visiting town. Rosemary, meet Glenn Reed and Mauricio Zambr… Zambrava?"

"Zambrano," Mauricio added, a little stiffly. He couldn't quite put his finger on it, but something about this young woman had him on his guard. Mauricio was not one for fashion, but she looked as though she'd stepped straight off the cover of a magazine. She wore a perfectly tailored black sheath dress, a sparkling silver necklace of some intricate design, and wrist-length cream-colored gloves. Her hair and makeup were exquisite, with nary a lash out of place.

The young woman turned, tilted her head, and graced them with a dazzling Hollywood smile. She extended her hand to Mauricio.

"Charmed," she said with a voice that was honey to the ears. Mauricio took her hand with the same caution as one might take a jaguar's paw. "Stanley tells me you are from Venezuela, Mr. Zambrano. When our business is finished you must tell me more of your country. I do so love hearing tales of exotic locales."

"Certainly, Miss Lavoie," Mauricio replied, with absolutely no intention of doing so.

She turned to Glenn. "And Mr. Reed, it's a pleasure to meet you as well."

Glenn took her offered hand listlessly. Mauricio noticed, to his astonishment, that his partner wasn't even looking at her. His gaze was once again fixed on Stanley's window, which presented a fantastic view of the beach and the tiniest sliver of sea.

"By a stroke of luck, Miss Lavoie happens to be in San Cicaro to see a friend and dropped by for a visit mere moments after you yourselves left. She's very interested in your pearls. Just don't ask her how she got her money, boys." Stanley's smile stretched his face as he took a satisfied sip of bourbon. "She won't tell me, and I don't think you've got what it takes to convince her."

"A woman must be allowed some secrets, mustn't she?" Rosemary purred. "It's really quite a boring story anyway, and I do so hate to be a bore."

She plucked the pearl that they'd left with Stanley off his desk and held it up to catch the light. "These, however… these are most certainly not boring. I am prepared to make what I feel to be a generous offer to take them off your hands."

She paused for a moment. "Although, it is a shame about the number. Stanley said you have just over thirty? Not nearly enough to make a proper necklace. Still, I have no doubt I shall devise something to do wi—"

"Would 88 be enough?" blurted Glenn suddenly.

Three heads turned to stare at him. Even Rosemary seemed taken aback, but she recovered quickly.

"Well, the average pearl necklace consists of 85 pearls. So that would be plenty, with a couple of extras for a pair of earrings, perhaps."

Glenn wordlessly reached into his pocket and pulled out a small bag. He upended it into Miss Lavoie's opened palm, and a waterfall of garibaldi-colored pearls spilled over into her ivory glove.

"That's 56," he said casually. "Mauricio has the rest."

As Rosemary laughed in delight and Stanley playfully chided Glenn for keeping him in the dark, Mauricio stared at his partner in stunned silence. A hurricane of emotions roiled within him—astonishment, anger, disappointment—but the most prominent was the acrid taste of betrayal. Glenn had lied. He'd gone back for more pearls. And he had left his partner out of the plan.

Mauricio stayed mostly silent during the negotiation, lest he let his anger dominate his words. It mattered little however, as Stanley argued the value and uniqueness of the pearls with Rosemary with considerable aplomb. Only when they had settled on a final price did Stanley seem to remember that it wasn't technically his deal to make, and he turned to Mauricio for confirmation.

Mauricio could only approve with a curt nod.

Hands were shaken and backs were clapped. A moment later, Rosemary cut two checks—one for Stanley, to cover the loan for the diving attraction, and a much larger one for Mauricio and Glenn. Stanley insisted on a celebratory drink for his diving partners. Mauricio reluctantly accepted, as Glenn continued to stare out the window with vacant eyes.

They departed Stanley's office ten minutes later. The bitter burn of bourbon had done little to quell Mauricio's anger. As they stepped out, Glenn made to wander away, until Mauricio clasped his shoulder in an iron grip.

"Where are you going?" he asked through gritted teeth.

"Hmm?" said Glenn listlessly. "Just taking a walk. Gonna go see the ocean, I think. It's nice at night, you know. Real nice."

"Just a harmless walk on the beach, is it? Not trying to get more pearls behind my back?"

Glenn didn't turn around, but his gaze slid upwards so that he was staring into the sky. "Ah, don't be mad, partner. We needed them pearls, didn't we? Needed the money."

"I told you it wasn't safe!"

"What's the harm? Just my own hide I was risking. Now, if you'll excuse me…" he gently lifted Mauricio's hand, removing it from his shoulder.

"Hey, you hang on," Mauricio commanded, grabbing Glenn's wrist. "I'm not done talking about this with you!"

His partner shrieked as though he'd been shot. Shocked, Mauricio released him immediately. Yet as Mauricio leapt back in surprise, his fingers caught on Glen's sleeve, revealing a few inches of skin. Before Glenn could cover it, Mauricio caught a glimpse of something embedded in the man's flesh.

"What is that?" asked Mauricio, dumbfounded. "Was that a piece of coral? Is it stuck in your wrist? By all that's holy, man, we have to get you to a hospital!"

"*No!*" said Glenn sharply. His eyes were no longer vacant, but wild and active. He backed away a few steps, hunched over like a cornered animal. "No! It's… it's nothing. Just a little piece. It'll push itself out in a few days. Like a splinter, you know?"

"Did that happen while you were diving? Must have hurt horribly in the saltwater. Is this what's had you so distracted?" Mauricio asked, sighing. He'd never been able to hold on to anger very well, his fury already slipping away. "Look, if you don't want to go to the hospital, maybe I can get it out. I have my dive knife back at the hotel, I could…"

Glenn turned and fled, vanishing into the night.

Mauricio stared after him. Should he chase his partner down? And do what, exactly? Force him to go to the hospital? Berate him further for the lie? Punch him once, just to feel better? All seemed equally pointless to Mauricio. With a sad shake of his head, he made his way back to the hotel.

Glenn's bed was still empty when Mauricio awoke the next morning. He rose, dressed quickly, and went to look for his partner.

The beach where they'd held their scuba demonstration was not far from the hotel, but it still took Mauricio a few minutes' solid running to reach it. To his considerable relief, the first thing he saw was the silhouette of a man sitting peacefully on the beach, backlit by the rising eastern sun.

His heart skipped a beat as he approached Glenn. Approaching, he noticed that Glenn was seated not on the beach itself, but in the surf, a foot of water lapping at his waist. When Mauricio was halfway across the beach, he realized that Glenn's silhouette was oddly lumpy and misshapen. And as he reached his partner's side, a chill ran through Mauricio's body the likes of which he had never known. As cold fear swept through him his vision hazed for a moment. He didn't trust himself not to faint in terror or vomit in disgust.

The entire right half of Glenn's body had sprouted vibrant, purple coral. It grew out of his flesh much as it did the sea floor, except that its structure was more of a vine than a shrub. Strands of coral emerged from different points on Glenn's body, coursed around him in thick, purple ropes as wide as Mauricio's wrists, before being embedded in his flesh again. Blood and chunks of viscera encircled each entry and exit point. Growths like arrowheads blossomed from Glenn's ruptured right eye, his windpipe, and the right side of his ribcage. The largest vine of them all snaked up his right arm and shoulder, before finally piercing the base of his skull.

Straight into his brain stem.

Mauricio must have made some involuntary noise, because what remained of the man's head slowly turned to look at him. The parasitic coral bent and twisted with the effort, but never broke.

"Partner," whispered Glenn. His voice rasped as though he'd been coughing his lungs out for a week, the coral protruding from his throat vibrated with every word. And yet, despite his horrible condition, Mauricio noticed that Glenn's left eye shone with total clarity. "I'm sorry… should have listened to you. Stayed away. Figured… few more pearls, pay off the loan. Profitable from day one. Dived at night. Corals glow in dark."

"It's okay, Glenn," Mauricio tried, choking on his voice. His partner went on.

"Made mistake. Dropped my rock… brushed coral. Piece got under my skin. Growing ever since."

"Okay," Mauricio managed in what he hoped was a reassuring manner. He wanted to look his partner in the eye, but couldn't force himself to look at the coral sprouting there, swaying as though caressed by an invisible breeze. "Come on, Glenn. Let's get you to a hospital. They've got all sorts of tricks these days, they'll get it out of you."

"Can't leave," Glenn murmured. "In my brain now. Coral's calling me to ocean. Can say no, but… just. It's, gonna win, partner. Make me… join, cemetery."

There was fear in Glenn's voice. A quiet fear, not the horror and dread that you'd expect from a torn man discussing his impending demise. There was a tear in his left eye.

"No," said Mauricio. "You're not going anywhere. What we're going to do then, is you're going to stay right there, and I'm going to go get a hammer, or a bat, and I'm going to break the coral. Then we can…"

"*No!*" Glenn's scream was as unearthly as it was desperate. "No… it'll fight. Stab… infect you too. Please… just, sit. Wait, with me. Partner."

Mauricio nodded mutely. He chose a spot a few feet to the right of Glenn and sat in the sea, saltwater soaking through his pants, gentle waves lapping at his legs. They looked out over the ocean. A trio of gulls flew overhead, their piercing cries the only sound to break the silence.

"Wish it was sunrise," Glenn croaked after a few minutes of silence. "Beautiful sunsets on, west coast. Buildings block sunrises, though."

"You can turn around. Might be able to see it." said Mauricio, his voice wavering. Yet he could see the coral stiffen further, the strands expand just a little. The suggestion was futile, and the pair sat in silence for a few more minutes.

"Don't wanna go," Glenn added, sobbing. "Ocean terrifies me. Don't belong there. Happy Mr. Gray funded… us. Ocean, all yours. Numbers, mine. Never have to go, in again."

And despite his anguish, Glenn managed one final, winning smile. "Was, *great* plan, right partner?"

"It was. It was a great plan," Mauricio agreed. He kept his eyes pinned on the ocean so that Glenn couldn't see his face.

Without warning, the coral won. Glenn pitched over and fell face first into the sea, coughing and sputtering as he inhaled salt water. His right arm reached forward, latched onto the sand, and dragged his body a few inches towards the depths.

The moment Glenn hit the water, Mauricio sprang into action. He grabbed the rock that he'd spotted three feet to his right—it was either his weight stone or one of Glenn's, he wasn't sure which—and leapt over to his partner's side. With one swift movement he bashed the stone at the thickest strand of coral, the one that stretched from wrist to head. The coral tore out of Glenn's skull with a sickening squelch, and the rock slipped from Mauricio's hands, splashing into the water a few feet away.

Mauricio himself lost his footing at the same time and crashed ungracefully into the waves. He scrambled away, rising to crouch and ready for a fight. It soon became clear that there was no point. His partner lay face up in the sea, blood leaking from the back of his head, his eyes wide and unseeing.

Glenn Reed was dead.

The San Cicaro Police Department had questions, of course, but not nearly as many as Mauricio had expected. To his relief, none of them seemed to even entertain the notion that Mauricio had anything to do with Glenn's death. All signs suggested some freak accident. Mauricio warned them not to touch the corals on the corpse, and they nodded and handled the body with the utmost care.

Mauricio had spent the first few moments after Glenn's death thoroughly checking over his own body, relieved when he found no wayward slivers of coral. Nevertheless he sat for many long minutes, alone with his partner's corpse, waiting for some invisible speck to rupture out of his skin. It never happened, and eventually he carefully dragged Glenn back out to the beach before asking a horrified jogger to get the police.

Stanley Gray must have seen the ruckus on the beach, for he was soon at Mauricio's side. His eyes held a deep sadness as he watched the police place a tarp over Glenn's mangled face.

"I am so sorry, Mr. Zambrano," he said quietly. He moved as though to place a hand on Mauricio's shoulder, but decided against it at the last moment. "Is there anything you need?"

"Yes," said Mauricio after a moment's thought. "A sign. Folk need to be warned that this beach isn't safe. Something simple, eye-catching. 'Do Not Swim', maybe."

Stanley nodded slowly.

"I think that can be arranged." The businessman looked out at the beach, where the advancing tide had already started to erase the blood stains in the sand. "Yes, I think that would be wise. Nothing ever washes up on this beach. Alive or dead. God almighty, it was so long ago I had forgotten…"

Mauricio's brow rose expectantly before Stanley spoke again.

"When I was a child, I had a neighborhood friend named Ralphie. He was the son of one of my father's friends, and we would play along this beach as our fathers drank together in town. Once we held a competition to see how long we could hold our breaths underwater. Ralphie won, but his knee was bleeding. He said he'd scraped it on some coral."

Stanley's mouth was a grim slash.

"His father told everyone that the scrape became infected and claimed Ralphie's life, but I knew differently. I snuck over to his room one night when his parents were asleep, and I looked in the window. He was tied to the bed. He looked… well, I suppose you can guess. I could hardly even recognize him anymore. In my horror, I fled without saying a word. The next morning his parents announced he had passed away." Stanley's gaze was distant with the memory. "I never told anyone. Thought I might have imagined it."

Will I become old enough to someday forget this? Mauricio thought as he too stared at the horizon. *Forget Glenn? Do I want to?*

"So what will you do now, Mr. Zambrano?" Stanley asked after a moment's silence. "Return to Venezuela? With the money from Miss Lavoie's check I believe you could be fiscally comfortable for quite some time. Live the life you wish and leave the diving to younger men."

Mauricio wanted to say yes. He wanted to tell Stanley that there was nothing for him in the United States anymore, and that it was time for him to return home. But the words caught in his throat, and instead he said nothing.

Stanley must have been waiting for a sign of hesitation, because he swiftly filled the silence. "Or, I have another offer that may tempt you."

He sat in the sand beside Mauricio. "Before you and Mr. Reed ever set foot in this city, I had already begun to pursue a way to introduce people to the wonders of the oceans of San Cicaro, albeit in a different way. I had envisioned a building, a hybrid aquarium and research center. Dozens of tanks, millions of gallons of water, and space for the scientists as well. Plans are already well underway. If you're willing, I would like you to join our staff."

Mauricio frowned. "Me? Are you sure?"

"Absolutely. You, Mr. Zambrano, have a skill set that we need. I have people who know money, people who know real estate, people who know marketing and media and public relations. And people in scientific circles, who professed intrigue after I had told them of your demonstration. You are the caliber of man we need now. Someone practical, practiced and reserved, who knows the sea, beauty and danger alike. Equally as important, I think you of all people may understand the motivation behind such a massive undertaking." Stanley scooped up a handful of sand and allowed it to fall between his fingers.

It came to Mauricio in a flash. "We bring the sea to them. People will never again need to go into the waters of San Cicaro. There will be no more Ralphies or Glenns."

"Precisely," said Stanley. "The public's curiosity will be slated, and maybe the scientists will be able to figure what's going on out there. So what do you say?"

Mauricio only needed a moment's thought.

Wordlessly he extended his hand. Stanley shook it.

Lunch Break

Olivia finished the story with a smile and leaned back. It was so *refreshing* to read about Stanley Gray and everything he did. Even though the aquarium was now shut down, it was heartening to know even back then, people were willing to invest so much into researching and preserving the ocean.

Checking her phone clock, she saw it was just past noon, a good time to take lunch. Yet as she moved to rise, a headline caught her eye.

Oldest Inmate in San Cicaro Sanatorium Dies

"Amnesia victim estimated to be over a hundred years old," Olivia read aloud, her eyes widening at the next line. "The cab driver who delivered him to the hospital said he was found wandering around what is now Sentimental Pines Park, wearing a priest's frock. Possessing no knowledge of his own name, the Sanatorium referred to him as 'Juan Perez.'"

That's it, Olivia realized, her memories clicking into place. *Sentimental Pines! That's where we used to hike.*

The rest of the article only added to the mystery. Police had interviewed the mission, thinking Juan might have been the priest who had gone missing there. Yet the clergy had claimed it was not the same man. Juan Perez had spoken an almost archaic form of Spanish, while the missing Father Andreas was perfectly fluent in English. The patient was also visibly older, by at least a decade.

A coincidence I guess... Olivia told herself. Yet she couldn't help but ponder if perhaps the man had a run-in with the Dark Watchers himself.

Hunger put an end to that idea, and she made her way to the elevator. Maybe she would go for tacos? She tried to remember if there was a good taco place nearby. She considered texting Keanu to ask, but remembered she hadn't read his previous message yet. She wracked her brain, trying to think of nearby lunch places. That's when she remembered the one place she always wanted to try, a place she had read about in the *Observer*. A place that happened to be only a few blocks away.

Golgonooza.

Olivia took a seat at the bar, plucking a menu propped up by the salt and pepper shakers. Her stomach sang for the mahi-mahi tacos, but her heart was set on something vegetarian. Perhaps the chipotle portobello and grilled corn tacos would suffice. Maybe some guacamole to help if it proved too spicy.

She didn't know how but the bartender was *there*, ready for her, welcoming and warm despite his bulk. "The cauliflower and cotija tacos are also great."

"Alright... I'll try them."

With that, he served her a glass of iced water and disappeared after entering the order. Alone with her thoughts, Olivia's gaze turned to the garish and wild local art that covered the entire restaurant. Some of it was portrayed upon canvas, while much of the rest was daubed directly on the walls themselves. A few seemed to portray some of the recent unexplained phenomena including faeries, animals with too much intelligence, and holes in the world.

Stylized hounds circled a patchwork beast of bones and stitched pelts on one graffitti fresco. On another, a pale woman tumbled through a landscape of tendrils and leering golden eyes. Rats with the faces of men peered up from sewer grates. Capering between each overlapping piece of surrealist art were shadowy fairies with moth wings and unsettling smiles. The fae led her attention to a man staring at a computer screen, which stared back at him through an ominous eye. It was like a Bosch painting for the modern age.

Olivia's gaze roved across this mural of punk rock madness, until her eyes settled on the patrons. A familiar face sat at the far side of the bar.

She was a compact woman, maybe of Hispanic heritage, with long hair. What was in her hair, catching the light, was what Olivia had noticed. Bullet shells, runes, Mahjong tiles, and a foil flower. She wore a t-shirt with a local band, Barrio Fantasma, and seemed utterly absorbed in the amber fluid she sloshed about in the vial before her.

I think it's her, Olivia realized. *That 'spiritual consultant' all over Youtube. Okay. Remember not to be too direct. Let's see, something to start an innocent conversation...*

"So… you a Barrio fan?" She immediately regretted letting the words out of her mouth, as if wearing their shirt wasn't obvious enough.

Xiomara smiled, and glanced at Olivia. Not in a lecherous way but certainly taking measure. She nodded her head at the bartender. "Ostrander there says they're awesome. I've never seen them. To be honest I just like the t-shirt and the name… Baaarrrioo Fan~taaas~ma."

"Yeah, they're pretty *fan*-tastic I've heard…" she said, immediately thinking, *Goddamnit, stop screwing this up.*

"A nice pair of blank canvases you got there," the consultant nodded towards her feet. It took Olivia a moment to realize what she was talking about.

"Oh right, the sneakers? Yeah, I guess they are pretty basic. Still, I guess this is the right place to have them punched up a bit?"

"Lots of local talent at the Golgonooza," she replied, pointing at the graffiti around them while looking Olivia full in the eyes. "But I'm guessing you work something a little more Dolly?"

"Dolly?"

"Nine to five."

Olivia laughed lightly. "You could say that. I'm a reporter."

"Another one," Xiomara said.

Olivia couldn't tell what she meant by that, her tone neither disdainful nor impressed. "Another?"

"Well, I used to work with a guy. Brezh Badac, ol' Brezzy of mine. Haven't heard from him in a while though. I hope he's doing alright."

Olivia had, in fact, run into the man. He had been working for the *Cicaro Inquirer*, and attended some professional happy hours. She didn't think much of the guy, and not just because he worked for the enemy. That haunted look of his was creepy, and the story went that he took a four month sabbatical before finally quitting his newspaper to move to San Francisco.

"Oh… he's probably fine," Olivia replied noncommittally.

"So, what're you working on? Or are you working on me for something?"

"First thing I'm going to work on is tacos."

"A girl with priorities."

"That's me." Olivia grinned, pointing two thumbs at herself. "But afterwards, research at the libraries. Cataloging old editions of the *San Cicaro Observer* for our archives."

"Watch out for that cute librarian," Xiomara grinned. "He's a heartbreaker, that one."

Olivia's confidence completely and totally fizzled into a flat, empty balloon. Scoring Keanu's phone number had been the highlight of her day, and now rumors had to crawl out of the shade. "I'll keep that in mind…"

Xiomara perked up, perhaps realizing her words had struck a nerve. "Umm. Can I buy you a drink?"

"Why?"

"Because you suddenly look like you need one. And black-spiced rum makes a better boyfriend."

Olivia cracked a weak grin, but shook her head. "I appreciate it, but I got to work after this. This isn't Boston, after all."

Ostrander returned with her tacos, and as Olivia browsed the hot sauce selection, she figured it might be easier to let Xiomara introduce herself. "So what's your name?"

"That would be one Xiomara Chivara. Though my friends call me Xio. Wanna be my friend?"

Having rehearsed this moment in her head, Olivia blinked and looked over at her. "Xiomara? Like that woman from those Youtube videos?"

"My reputation precedes me," the consultant tucked some hair behind her ear, a bullet casing jangling as she did. "Xiomara, fixer of the spirits. Reluctant savior. Fake celebrity. Anti-influencer and bane of landlords. But something tells me you knew that the moment you sat down."

Busted, Olivia thought. "Well, I didn't want to assume. Might end up with a fake signature."

"A wise call. So, what's the interest? Pleasure or business?"

In truth, Olivia hadn't gotten that far. While Xiomara might be a good interview candidate for a puff piece on a slow day, there was no guessing how Marco or Melissa would want to spin it. "A little of both, maybe. Have you ever heard of folks called the Dark Watchers?"

"There's a blast from the past. The last guy who knew about them died ages ago. Said something about them being… not evicted, but rather pushed out." Xiomara shrugged. "Nothing draws a crowd like a crowd."

"A crowd?" Olivia asked. It was a simple trick, an open-ended question that lets people prattle on.

"Well, not as of late," Xiomara said with a frown. "Business hasn't been booming recently. Like the deep breath before the barbaric yawp."

Olivia blinked, unsure how to process that answer. "Well, how about some… questions about the past? You seem knowledgeable about esoteric and forgotten things."

"That's a brooooooooad subject. Anything in particular?"

One thing immediately sprang to mind as Olivia gathered her first taco. "Have you heard about the oldest inmate who died at the nearby mental hospital, back in the 50's? Was like, a hundred years old?"

"The guy dressed in the priest's frock? Spoke only Spanish?"

"*Mmph!*" Olivia's surprise wasn't just at Xiomara's knowledge, but at how cheesy the tacos were. A thin string slapped her on the cheek as she drew back her bite. She nodded, wiping her face with her knuckles.

"Juan Perez is a nobody. But Father Andreas? There's a name that pops up here and there, usually with a good story," Xiomara scratched her chin, ponderously. "It was said he wasn't the start of it, but he was... what's the chemistry term? Catalyst?"

"Huh?"

"Or maybe the pin in the grenade. There was always a little bit of magic to this town, but it was clogged. Somewhere. After Perez died, things started to get crazy again. Maybe it's just taking this long to catch up, like how hard the ground remains after winter has gone bye-bye."

Get crazy again? Olivia pondered that as she finished her first taco. "Like, what, increasingly? Exponentially?"

"Well, more like ocean waves. Sometimes, they cancel each other out, but other times they converge and are more powerful. I think the former is what's going on now."

Stopping herself from taking another bite, Olivia thought long and hard over what that meant. "You um... you know people I can talk to about this? Maybe get to the bottom of some old mysteries in this town?"

"Sure do, hon. Everyone knows a piece of the puzzle, but from where we stand we can only see how a few parts snap together. Someone has to look down from above to grasp the picture. Maybe a reporter can do just that."

Suspecting she was being angled, Olivia bit. "And I suppose you're willing to answer some questions in that regard? Maybe agree to an interview later?"

"Only if you agree to the rules."

"Let's hear 'em." Olivia said as she started on the last taco.

"Well, we'll start with getting me guacamole. And maybe tacos later for dinner. No pictures, no video but you can record. When I say we're done, that's all folks. And we get to do the switcheroo, where I ask questions back at you." Xiomara finished her drink with a flourish.

As long as she doesn't order carne asada over lobster, I guess I can swing that, Olivia thought. "Is that all?"

"There are other rules, but they only come up if you cross a boundary. Leave a good tip too, Ostrander is a growing boy."

The bartender gave Xiomara a doubtful look, rubbing his belly.

Olivia nodded and placed her phone on the bar. "Digits?"

Xiomara reached into her jacket and slid a business card over that read "consultant." Olivia entered it into her phone before sending a message with her own contact info. Xiomara winked as her jacket buzzed upon the text's arrival. "Now, no calls past my bedtime."

"And when is that?" Olivia asked innocently.

"Call me and find out."

Olivia laughed nervously, suddenly realizing that this woman might have been flirting with her this entire time. True to her word though, Olivia made sure to leave a solid 20% for Ostrander. Yet as she turned to go, she realized Xiomara was staring at her curiously. Perhaps even in a concerned way.

"Ummm, are you okay?"

"Yeah, just… got a feeling. There's a glimmer around you." Xiomara made a gesture with her hand, and Olivia could only guess at the meaning. The consultant reached into her hair and unwound one of the Mahjong tiles, sliding it towards the reporter. Olivia glanced at the image of a flower with five petals, surrounded by vines.

"The plum flower, a symbol of perseverance and hope. And transitoriness. Go on, keep it. I think you'll need the luck."

Olivia checked Xiomara's hair, and wondered how it managed to be so tangled and yet clean. Accepting the tile with a nod, Olivia stood. "I'll be in touch."

"You'd better."

Keanu was gone when she returned, replaced by a grumpy old woman who eyed her wearily. Although not thrilled with the old librarian's disapproving glare, it was less awkward than meeting the young playboy again.

With a heaving sigh, the older librarian let her back into the elevator, and soon enough Olivia sat in front of the microfiche reader again. Instead of diving back into work however, she decided to procrastinate by checking her email. There was nothing on her work account, but her personal one sported a message from Melissa, which arrived only a moment ago.

> Hey superstar. I was wondering if you could make sure you copy a particular news article for me while you're there. I know it was during October, November or December of 1957. Something about US military intelligence operating in San Cicaro's suburbs during the Cold War. It would have been a front or second page story, so it shouldn't be too hard to find.
>
> Keep this between the two of us, will you? No reason to worry Marco.

Checking her list, Olivia realized there were no editions around that date she was supposed to find. Surely, if they already copied it, it would be in the digital archives for Melissa to fetch herself?

Unless there was something else going on.

Moonshot
Ichabod Ebenezer

Anthony peered out from behind the trashcans, scouting for the outlaw. His twitchy hand rested on his Wild Bill Hickok cap gun, the smell of gunpowder still lingering from the last paper roll. Anthony spotted his foe, half a block away behind the big green dumpster of the O.K. Corral.

"Ike Clanton," Anthony mustered with all the authority of an 11-year-old, "throw down your gun and come out, or I'm coming in, guns blazing!"

"I don't wanna throw out my gun, and I don't wanna be Ike Clanton anymore," Max called back, his wimpy tone causing the O.K. Corral to vanish. In its place stood the less prestigious Vista Nueva apartments of boring old San Cicaro.

"Come on, Max. Someone has to be Ike Clanton. And you're supposed to say, 'You'll never take me alive!'"

"Maybe I can be Wyatt Earp next time," Max said.

"You asked for it—I'm coming in!" Anthony shouted, breaking into a dash towards the dumpster, pulling the trigger over and over. *Pak! Pak! Pak!*

"Fine, I'm dead," Max said, completely unphased as his brother gunned him down. "Can I be Earp now?"

Anthony slowed, groaning in disappointment. Before he could berate his brother, Mama called out, "Boys! Come inside. Papi's home!"

Max jumped up and ran past him, but Anthony was three years older and a lot faster. He gave his little brother a shove as he sped past and threw open the screen door. The old spring sang as it opened and brought the door back with a *whack* just before Max got there.

The Reyes house was small. The half-bathroom to Anthony's left smelled of Aunt Araceli's beauty products and dampness. Off to his right was a modest bedroom where Grandpa and Nani slept. They used to sleep in the little addition Grandpa had built as a second floor, until his war injuries made going up the stairs challenging. Uncle Chencho slept there now, but with Papi back from farmhand work out in the countryside, that was about to change too.

Alex followed the sound of voices down the short hallway into the family room where he and Anthony slept. During the farming season, Mama slept there with them. Anthony would miss her company, but he missed Papi more.

"Papi!" Anthony called.

"He's in the kitchen, where did you think?" Grandpa said from behind his newspaper.

An archway to the left opened into the kitchen and dining room, where Bisa and Nani spent their days. At more than ninety-years-old, Bisa sat on her usual stool between the refrigerator and stovetop wearing an apron and holding a wooden spoon. She didn't cook anymore, so no one knew what the apron was for. Yet the wooden spoon would still whack anyone who got too greedy with a meal that wasn't done yet.

Papi was standing by the table, smiling broadly with a corn husk-wrapped tamale in his hand.

"Papi!" Anthony jumped up into his arms. Moments later, he felt Max's arms around his legs as his little brother bounced excitedly and hugged them both.

"¡Ay, mis hijitos! ¡Que rápido están creciendo!"

"English," Grandpa said from the other room.

Papi chuckled, looking past his kids at his father's newspaper. When Grandpa came up from Mexico, America had been the land of dreams, but he quickly learned that nobody handed you the good life. Yet all the employers, or their clients, spoke English, so he taught himself by reading discarded newspapers and listening to English radio stations. He spoke it every chance he got and in a few short years, he was the one bossing the other workers.

He always said he wasn't afraid his kids would lose touch with the community. "People will use every excuse to say you are not American, but nobody is going to say you aren't Mexican."

"You are both so big. Let me look at you," Papi said, holding them at arm's length to study them. Anthony looked away, feeling a little embarrassed, and saw Mama, smiling with wet eyes. She hadn't smiled like that since Papi's short visit before school.

"Are you going to stay longer this time?" Max asked the question Anthony had in his heart.

"The growing season is over, *m'ijo*," Papi said, mussing up Max's hair. "I'm going to stay so long, you're going to get sick of me."

Papi turned his attention to Anthony and touched the yellow paper star on his chest.

"What's this?" Papi asked. "They made you sheriff, Antonio?"

As Anthony looked down, Papi flicked the cowboy hat off his head.

"Oh, Papi." Anthony rolled his eyes.

"Did you get paid?" Mama asked.

Papi stood and dug a roll of bills out of his back pocket. "Yes, and we are going to celebrate tonight!"

Grandpa was in his boxers and t-shirt, poking at the flank steak sizzling on his little Coleman grill and smoking his nasty cigarettes. Mama came out with a tray of butter-drenched corn and sliced bell peppers, setting it on an old orange crate next to the grill. Papi's singing echoed through the open bathroom window, competing with the *música norteña* pumping out of the neighbor's radio.

Max found a feather, which Bisa said belonged to a condor. "When I was a *niña*, my grandmother told me how the men used to sew condor feathers into their clothes. The spirit of Condor granted them protection in battle and blessed their ceremonies."

Max stuck the feather into a paper headband he wore, and the pair played Cowboys and Indians for a while. But Anthony soon grew bored, as Max cried out every time he was shot, "You missed me 'cause of the feather!"

"You two need to get cleaned up as soon as Papi is out of the shower," Mama said, heading up to the loft with clean sheets.

"Yes, Mama," Anthony said.

The sun burned orange as it edged closer to the ocean below, and everyone brought chairs and tables to the lawn of the apartments a few doors down. Laughter and loud Spanish conversations filled the air between songs.

"Honey!" Grandpa yelled. He was holding the flank steak up by his long fork. "Meat's ready!"

Bisa's carnitas were a favorite of the community. Everyone still called them "Marisol's carnitas" even though Nani had been making them for as long as Anthony could remember. It was Bisa's recipe, and she watched her daughter with the keen eye of a condor while Nani did all the work.

Nani came out and took Grandpa's fork along with the steak. She paused long enough to tell Anthony, "Start bringing chairs to the Huerta's place," then disappeared back inside.

Anthony holstered his gun and ferried chairs over to Mrs. Huerta at the apartments one by one. The other kids were running around on the lawn, kicking a ball back and forth. Anthony hurried with the chairs so he could play with them before anyone made him take care of Max.

Soon, the tables were set. Each family brought out their favorite dishes and everybody ate like it was the Fourth of July. The Tac family from down the street sent their regrets, but also a dish of Leila's rice pudding for all to enjoy. October was the best time for corn, and Mama's *elotes* were one of Anthony's favorite things in all the world. That and Mrs. Bonales' *arroz con leche*, but he would never tell Bisa that.

There were *chicharrones* and *pollo asado*, apples with chili powder, *papas fritas* and pinto bean soup. Everyone was happy and well fed, and there were many toasts to the men who returned from the farms.

The tables filled up as the evening turned to night, and just when they thought the food might run out, more appeared. Uncle Chencho joined their table when his job at the construction site let out, and later on Aunt Ari arrived with her current boyfriend.

After dinner, they turned up the radio, and the men danced with their wives. Even Grandpa got up and stomped his feet while Nani twirled her skirts and stepped around him. Anthony couldn't remember when he'd last seen them so happy. When *El Perico Loro* came on the men joined in with their best *gritos*. Anthony caught Max's eye from across the table, and both of them threw back their heads and cried joyfully into the night.

The music went on for hours while Chencho lamented losing the privacy of the upstairs room. Secretly, he told Anthony, "It will be good to share the family room with you and Max again. I only take the bedroom because it is expected of me."

Anthony smiled at this, but Max hid his face. He always missed having Mama there at first, but he'd get used to it.

"We interrupt this program to bring you this news flash," a man said in English over the radio.

The group quieted down to listen, but that initial statement was only followed by odd, regular beeping like in those *Space Patrol* radio shows. Anthony used to enjoy listening to them, but ever since the Huertas got a television, he'd fallen in love with the Westerns.

The beeping stopped, and the man's voice came back on. "That was the sound of Sputnik, the world's first artificial satellite. Launched by the Soviets, it is currently orbiting overhead at eighteen-thousand miles per hour. We do not have visual details to provide at this time, however this man-made moon is described as 23 inches in diameter and 185 pounds. Its contents are deemed classified. While the United States has officially extended its congratulations, this represents a major leap forward for Soviet scientists, one which beats American efforts by months, perhaps years. We now return you to your regularly scheduled programming."

The music came back, but *Señor* Vázques, who had been standing next to the radio, switched it off. The party fell into stunned silence. Anthony didn't understand why they were so upset, but he knew enough to shush Max when he started another *grito*.

"The Commies beat us," someone said.

"What's stopping them from nuking us right now?" someone else asked.

Nani crossed herself and Mama shushed the man, covering Anthony's ears, but the damage had been done. His skin prickled with cold sweat.

"What are we going to do?" Mrs. Reyes asked, and the tables erupted into heated Spanish argument. Grandpa's rules about speaking English held no sway with the other families, and even he joined in.

Anthony watched them, catching more of the emotion than the actual arguments, and he would have to ask Uncle Chencho later what some of the words meant. But he knew what nuke meant. It meant a really big bomb. He didn't understand a lot of the arguments, but something bad had happened. Some people thought they should prepare for an invasion, and someone else said they should learn to speak Russian.

The only thing everyone agreed on was that America had to beat the Commies to the moon.

Max woke and rubbed the crusties from his eyes. He found Anthony halfway through breakfast, and he rushed to catch up. His big brother was in a hurry to get out back as usual, but something had changed in Anthony.

"Can I *please* be Wyatt Earp today?" Max pleaded. It wasn't fair that he always had to be the bad guy and get shot.

"We're not playing cowboys today. Come on," Anthony said, walking up the slight incline of the alley.

"We're supposed to stay where we can hear Mama when she calls us," Max said, stopping just past the apartment trashcans.

Anthony turned around, but didn't come back. "Max, it's time to stop playing. We have to do something or else the Commies are going to win and they're going to invade America and we're going to have to learn Russian. If they don't just bomb us all."

Max curled his arms to his chest, worried. "How are we gonna stop them, Anthony?"

"You and me are going to build a rocket and get to the moon first. We're gonna show those Commies not to mess with America."

"But I don't know how to build a rocket," Max said, scratching his head.

"Remember when Uncle Chencho took us to the construction site to see the big trucks? They had all sorts of wood and stuff from the old buildings they were tearing down. They're just gonna throw it away. We can build a rocket out of that. We built a car out of cardboard and roller skate wheels. How hard can a rocket be?"

"Okay, but shouldn't we ask Mama?"

"If we ask Mom, she might say no. This is too important. You don't wanna be a Commie, do you?"

"No," Max said, not really knowing what that meant, but feeling pretty sure it was bad.

"Then come on. It's not too far, and you've got to help me carry stuff."

Anthony turned around again, and Max hurried to catch up.

The construction zone was a two-block section on the outskirts of the Mission District, and a few blocks up the hill from the Reyes' house. They passed the old adobe church that gave the city its name. Max stopped to run his fingers over the raised letters of the historical marker, which according to Aunt Ari said, "The bastards can never knock it down."

Immediately surrounding Mission San Cicaro was a pedestrian zone lined with street vendors during the day, and homeless people once the sun went down. One block further up the hill stood the chain link fences that surrounded the construction zone.

A drawing of parks and high-rise office buildings was bolted to the fence, proclaiming a future of prosperity, but spray paint covered the board. "¡Viva La Raza!" and "You are tearing down our heritage!"

Max could recognize all the letters, but had to sound out the words. Anthony got impatient before Max got through the first slogan.

"Come on," Anthony commanded. Two sections of fence were held together with a chain, but Anthony easily squeezed between them.

"Are you sure we can take this stuff?" Max said as he stepped through and looked around the site.

A backhoe sat idle nearby, with its bucket piercing the roof of a small house. Bulldozer tracks led across the bare dirt to a large pile of earth with long wooden beams and wires sticking out all over.

"Does it look like they're using it?" Anthony answered. He picked up a malformed sheet of aluminum, one side covered in flaking, sunbaked paint. "This can be our nose cone."

That image fired Max's imagination, and he started picking up pieces of wood until he found a rough square of plywood. "We can make tail fins out of this!"

"Yeah! That's it, Maxy! We just need a couple more," Anthony said, taking it from him and putting it in a pile with the nose cone.

The two of them spent the next hour dragging over pieces of scrap metal and two-by-fours. Max wiped sweat off his forehead after dragging another plywood board to the pile. During a break, he gazed through a gap between the buildings that went all the way down to the ocean. The Ferris wheel on the boardwalk was going up, and Max remembered a flier for the Fall Festival. He could just about hear the calliope music, smell the popcorn, and taste the candy apples. If he was lucky, Anthony would forget about this rocket thing and the two of them could beg Papi to take them tomorrow.

Anthony waved at Max excitedly with some ducting he had found. If Max brought up the fair now, all he would do is make Anthony angry. He would wait until they got home. He looked at the pile of wood and metal they'd collected so far.

"How are we gonna get all this home, Anthony?" he asked.

Anthony poked his head over the broken adobe wall between them. "Maybe we can put it on the nose cone piece and drag that down the hill."

"Don't we have enough yet?"

"Almost. Our spaceship needs wires. And a button for launch. I found some switches for the dashboard." He held up a couple light switches.

"Keen!" Max smiled. "I saw some wires in that big dirt pile!"

"Don't get hurt," Anthony called after him as he ran.

"I won't!" Max yelled back just as his foot broke through the dirt, almost making him trip. "I'm okay!"

He looked down through the hole in the crumbled mud brick where his foot had just been. It was small and curiously deep, at odds with the haphazard, junkyard feel of the rest of the construction site.

"There's gophers here," Max told his brother. But with his next step, the ground fell away and Max went with it, screaming.

"Maxy!" Anthony yelled.

Max hit a floor of clay tiles some eight feet below, knocking the wind out of him. Dirt and pebbles continued to rain down on him, filling the one shaft of light from above with swirling dust.

"Max!" Anthony called above, and Max heard his running footsteps.

Max still couldn't talk or breathe, and tears made tracks down his face while mud caked his newly split lip. Was he going to die? What if he never got his breath back?

But he didn't die, and his breath slowly returned in noisy sobs. Anthony's worried face appeared in the hole above him. "Oh, thank God, Max! Why didn't you answer me?"

"Huuuhh... can't breathe," Max said. "Huuuhh! Huuuhh!"

Anthony reached a hand into the hole, but there was too much space between them. He shook his head as he spoke, "I'm going to get dad."

"No!" Max called back, catching his breath at last. "We'll get in trouble."

"We're *in* trouble, Max. We need grown-ups." His face disappeared from the hole above.

Max was suddenly aware of the darkness all around him, and heard the sounds of earth crumbling. He imagined the whole thing falling on top of him, crushing the life out of him. "Don't leave me!"

Anthony's footfalls faded into the distance.

Max stood in the lone beam of light, hugging himself to keep his arms out of the darkness. Water dripped somewhere and echoed all around. The whole place smelled like the dead earthworm Anthony had once shoved in his face.

Something skittered in the distance. Max imagined giant rats with glowing red eyes.

"*Anthony!*" he yelled, fear heightening his tone, but his brother was gone.

More movement startled him, like the scrape of glass against concrete. Max spun to face it, but couldn't see beyond the tip of his nose.

"Who's…" He couldn't finish the question. His throat was too dry to swallow, and his mouth was covered in dirt.

More movement to his right, and Max spun again. Yellow eyes stared back at him, circling in the darkness just beyond the solitary beam from above. A wolf's snout pushed into the light, lip curling, revealing pointed teeth.

Max found his voice and screamed. He backed away instinctively, but still stayed in the light.

The eyes and teeth grew closer, and Max could see the wide brim of a hat above the eyes.

"Did I scare you?" an old man's voice said from the darkness. He stepped closer, revealing more of himself. There was no snout, no wolf's teeth, no yellow eyes. It was just a man, with dark, weathered skin in a loose linen shirt and a dusty vest. A bolero hat sat upon his long gray hair, with a band of animal teeth. A silvery wolf's head adorned a necklace between the lapels of his vest.

Max turned to face him as the man circled, sticking to the shaft's penumbra, never close enough to be fully visible. Though he couldn't say why, the man scared Max enough that he didn't want to speak.

"You took a nasty fall," the man continued. His voice held concern, but there was danger in his eyes.

Had Anthony only just left? Max hoped he was on his way back already. If he were on the surface, he would have run from the man, but there was nowhere to go down here, nowhere to escape. There was only the light and the shadows.

"Was that your brother who just left you here? It isn't safe you know. Predators everywhere. It's lucky I was nearby." The old man laughed, a high-pitched barking giggle that did nothing to ease Max's mind.

"Who are you," Max asked, his voice shaking.

"Oh, so you do speak." The man put his fingers in his vest pockets. "The name I always liked best is Grandfather, so that is what you may call me."

"I already have a grandfather," Max said. The man giggled again.

"I bet you I'm older. Your grandfather could call me grandfather too." The man did look older than Grandpa, maybe even older than Bisa.

"What are you doing down here?" Max asked. The man hadn't hurt him yet, and he was keeping his distance. Perhaps he wasn't so dangerous.

"I have lived here a long, long time. The real question is what are you doing here?"

"I was looking for wires, and I fell. Me and my brother are gonna build a rocket." The old man's eyes glinted, and Max didn't like the hunger he saw there.

"A rocket? You know those are dangerous. Kaboom." He held up his fists, opening them and splaying his arms wide. Max couldn't help imagining that happening to him. He swallowed past his dusty throat.

"It's not a real one. Just pretend. We're gonna go to the moon before the Commies get there."

"The moon..." the old man said. For the first time, he looked away from Max. He stopped circling, turning his head toward the hole above them.

"Yeah. The moon. There was this show on the radio one time where men went to the moon, and there were these women living there who captured them, but the Moon Queen fell in love with one of them." Max swallowed. "I hope that doesn't happen to us."

"Oh, she sure is a harsh mistress. I once carried the moon in a box I held between my teeth," the old man said wistfully, still looking toward the distant sky.

"Maxy!" Papi's voice called from the world above.

"Papi!" Max yelled. More dirt fell from above, loosened by his voice. It fell into his open eyes, blinding him. He turned his face away and rubbed at them.

"Good luck with your rocket."

Max turned, startled at the direction the voice came from. He blinked, but only managed to make mud of the dust.

"Don't go! My dad can pull you out too," Max said stretching out his hand to find the man.

"No thanks, kid. I like to make my own way."

Max rubbed at his eyes, blinking again, but still unable to see more than a blur.

"Something to remember me by, kid." Max felt the old man's whispered words on his ear.

The blur resolved itself into the silver necklace, dangling in front of his face. Max reached out for it, catching one last sight of the old man's yellow eyes as he backed into the darkness again.

The light dimmed, and more dirt fell as Papi's face filled the hole above. "*M'ijo*, are you okay down there?"

"My lip is all swole."

Papi laughed. "Your lip is swole? How about you come up here where we can look at it?"

Uncle Chencho was there too, and the two men lowered a rope for Max, as Papi instructed him. "Put the loop around your waist and sit in it. We'll pull you up."

"Okay," Max said. He reached for the rope, but he still had the necklace in his hand. It was too big for his pockets, so he put it on before climbing into the loop of rope.

"Hey Maxy?" the old man's voice called from the darkness.

Max looked for the source of his voice, finally spotting those yellow eyes.

"You really shouldn't tell anyone about me, Max. No one will ever believe you."

"You ready, Maxy?" Uncle Chencho called.

Max tore his gaze away from the yellow eyes and nodded. Papi pulled him up while his uncle watched the rope. The old man was gone, leaving impenetrable darkness.

Papi hugged Max as soon as he was out.

"What were you boys doing up here anyway?" Uncle Chencho asked.

Anthony spoke before Max had to, looking at his shoes instead of meeting anyone's eyes. "We needed stuff so we can build a rocket and beat the Commies to the moon. It was my idea."

"I was looking for wires," Max added.

"Come on," Papi said. "Let's get home and wash you up."

"Wait!" Anthony looked up, eyes wide, as he pointed at the pile of wood and metal they'd collected. "What about our stuff for the rocket?"

Uncle Chencho laughed. "I'll bring it back home for you, and I'll get you some wires too. And if you need anything else, I'll get that too. You two don't come back here, alright?"

Just as they began to set off, Papi noticed the necklace on Max's chest. "Huh, *m'ijo*, where'd you get this?"

Max heard the old man's voice again, not in his memory, but as if he were speaking in Max's ear. *"Don't tell anyone about me, Max. No one will believe you."*

"I found it," was all Max could think to say. "Down there."

"Well," Papi said, scratching his scalp. "Finder's keepers I suppose. Let's get you home and have that lip looked at."

Anthony awoke the next day to the sound of knocking. He sat up, rubbing the sleep from his eyes. The familiar sound and smell of *chilaquiles* frying helped him to his feet, and he went to the front door to answer it.

No one was there, but while he was puzzling over that, the banging came again. It wasn't knocking, it was hammering. He pushed open the screen and saw Max on the lawn with Uncle Chencho's hammer and a hexagonal frame.

"Maxy?" Anthony asked, rubbing his eyes again.

Nani called from the kitchen. "He's been out there for the last hour, banging away. I thought you were going to sleep through everything."

Bisa rapped on the counter with her wooden spoon and scolded Nani in Spanish words Anthony had never learned.

"I am not going to burn them," Nani said, but she flipped her tortillas and stirred the tomato sauce anyway. "Tell Max to come in and eat breakfast. Then you two can go back outside."

"Max. Come have breakfast," Anthony called out.

Max continued hammering away, though he did more to bend the nail over than to drive it into the wood.

"Maxy!" Anthony tried again, but there was still no reaction. Anthony walked outside, remembering his bare feet only when the dew-soaked grass chilled them. He touched Max's shoulder, and Max spun around, hammer raised.

For a moment, Max's eyes were unfamiliar, then he blinked and his posture sagged. Max smiled.

"Hi, Anthony. Look how much I did already."

Two hexes built from two-by-fours were nailed to each end of the wooden panel Uncle Chencho had sawed down the day before. Anthony's "blueprint" lay in the grass nearby, soaked through, but the crayon drawing of the rocket and his parts list was clearly visible.

"That's good, Maxy. Nani says to come inside and eat."

"Okay. Hey! Maybe after breakfast, you can hold the nose cone on one end, and I'll bang it into shape. I'm good at banging."

"Sure Maxy. But I want to do the walls."

Max dropped the hammer on the lawn and the two boys went inside, washed up, and sat at the kitchen table. Nani put plates in front of them with the fried tortilla drenched in tomato sauce, then placed a fried egg on top.

"What's this, Max?" she asked, curling a finger under the necklace he wore.

Max jerked away from her. "It's mine. I found it at the construction site. Papi said it was fine."

Max hadn't let Anthony touch it yet either. Anthony wasn't jealous or anything, but he did want to see it. "I don't even like Indian stuff, but it's pretty nifty 'cause there's a wolf on it."

Bisa leaned forward on her stool, pulling her glasses off the top of her head to see it better. "Let me see that, Maxy."

Max covered it protectively, like he thought she would keep it. It was the same look he'd given Anthony, but this was worse because it was Bisa.

Bisa wasn't offended though, she smiled instead. "I'm sorry. *May* I see it, Maxy?"

Max put on a sour face, but he got up from his chair and took the necklace off. Bisa held the necklace and tilted her head back to look through the bottom half of her glasses. "This is not a wolf, Anthony. This is Coyote."

Max bounced on the balls of his feet, eager to reclaim it. She placed her glasses back in her hair and handed the necklace to him. "Take good care of that, Maxy. It is very old."

Max quickly slipped it around his neck and returned to his seat.

Bisa got comfortable on her stool, and Anthony knew a story was coming. He liked Bisa's stories almost as much as her cooking. Uncle Chencho sat down next to Anthony, and Nani served him a plate of chilaquiles.

"California is a funny place, Anthony. My mother was a young woman already before it was part of America. This was Mexico back then, and everyone who lived here was Mexican. But my grandmother remembered before it was Mexico. When she grew up, this was part of Spain. And what's even funnier is that *her* grandmother remembered before the Spanish got here and built Mission San Cicaro. She told my grandmother her stories, and my grandmother told them to me. The people who lived here then were called 'Ohlone,' but the Spanish called them Indians. Isn't it funny that you can live in the same place, and depending upon when, you can be called Indian or American?"

Anthony swallowed a huge mouthful. "No way, Bisa. You mean your great-great-grandmother was an Indian?"

"Ohlone. Yes, *mi niño*."

"No way," Anthony said again. In his mind, Indians were the bad guys. It was unimaginable that his ancestor was one.

"It's true, Antonio," Uncle Chencho said, accepting a tamale from Nani. "Those houses at the construction site are where they used to live."

"Where *I* lived when I was a *pequeña*," Bisa said. "Coyote lived there too."

Max's head perked up. "Coyote, like my necklace? He did?"

"Coyote is very important to the Ohlone people. They say he was there at the very beginning when the seas drained and the Earth was revealed beneath. He married the first woman and made her pregnant, so all the Ohlone call him Grandfather."

Max was holding that necklace again, his thumb rubbing against the silver head of Coyote, but he turned away from Bisa. "Hey, Anthony. Remember that war movie we watched and they had dice hanging in the cockpit for luck? I was thinking we could hang my necklace in the rocket. That way it can be for both of us."

His sudden desire to share came as a surprise to Anthony. Not that he was jealous or anything, but it would be fun to share the necklace. "Okay, Maxy. That would be swell."

Max shoveled the rest of his food in his mouth and stood up. "Thanks for the food Nani and Bisa. I'm gonna go work on the rocket now."

Before they could respond, he zoomed off with his arms outstretched as if someone had lit his fuse. Anthony hurried with his own food, not wanting Max to work on the rocket without him.

"Uncle Chencho, since it's Sunday, do you think you can cut the tail pieces for us? Mama won't let me use your saw."

"Sure Anthony. I'll be out in a little bit."

Anthony put his plate in the sink, kissed Nani and Bisa, and ran outside, the screen door slamming behind him.

They worked on the rocket until Mama called them in to get cleaned up for boring old church. As soon as they came home, they were back to hammering. Aunt Araceli sat out with them around sunset and wove clover flowers into bracelets and talked to them while they worked. Papi and Grandpa brought out chairs and sat on the lawn drinking beer and watching the rocket come together.

Mama came out again sometime after dark. "Enough building for today. Get cleaned up for dinner and bed."

Araceli came over and hugged Max. "You know, you worked really hard today. I have some red paint at home. Everybody knows red cars go faster, so… I wonder if the same is true for red rockets."

"What do you say, Max? I bet it would fly real fast," Anthony said.

"Can we, Aunt Ari?" Max asked.

"Maybe some black paint too?" Anthony added.

She kissed his forehead. "I'll bring it tomorrow morning."

Anthony woke in the middle of the night. For a moment, he thought someone else was there. He saw yellow eyes in the darkness, but they faded like the remains of a dream. Then he heard Max whispering, and Anthony rolled toward him.

Max was holding his necklace up, the coyote head shining in the moonlight that passed through a gap in the curtains.

"How did the moon get in the box though?" Max asked. Anthony didn't hear any response, but Max listened intently, then said, "Oh. Then what happened?"

"Who are you talking to?" Anthony asked.

Max jumped when Anthony spoke, but soon realized who it was. "Grandfather. He stole the moon so people would have light."

Anthony looked around the room, but Grandpa wasn't there. Just the two of them and Uncle Chencho laying half out of his blankets on the couch.

"Go back to sleep, Max. You're dreaming."

Max put the necklace back on and lay down. Eventually, Anthony drifted off again, but as he was shifting into dreams, he heard his brother whispering again.

Only this time, in his half-asleep state, Anthony heard someone whispering back.

He sat up, fear sending a chill through him. The family room was gone, replaced by a desert landscape. A campfire burned in front of him, and large rocks stood in a circle around the campfire. Max was gone. Uncle Chencho was gone.

An old man in a bolero hat and a dusty vest sat across the fire from Anthony. He wore Max's necklace and there was something wrong with his eyes.

Anthony pulled his blanket up to his chin as though it would protect him. The fire leapt and crackled, casting fleeting shadows upon the stones that surrounded them. The old man's shadow broke from the others and raced from stone to stone around the circle. It disappeared behind Anthony and a voice spoke in his ear.

"Men did not die in the first times."

Anthony flinched, looking for the source of the voice, and it continued in his other ear. "But far to the east, the Caddo peoples remember how I soon took care of that."

The shadow darted away, crossing each stone until it stopped behind the old man, growing larger until the entire stone stood in darkness. The old man smiled, revealing teeth like a wolf.

"Who are you?" Anthony tried to ask, but with fear gripping his chest, it only came out as a whisper.

The old man seemed to hear him anyway. His shadow spoke for him. "You can call me Grandfather."

"You are not my grandfather."

Giggling shadows appeared on all the stones, causing the hair on Anthony's arm and neck to stand up.

"Maybe not directly. But your father had a grandfather, and that's your great-grandfather. And kid, I'm the greatest one there is."

Anthony swallowed hard, but said nothing.

"The people lived forever, but more were born all the time. Even they realized they would run out of food. They came to me for my wisdom, and I told them that they should die much like animals."

The shadows upon the rocks took the shape of people who all clutched their throats and fell over.

"They did not like this, but saw the wisdom in it. They decided that people should die, but they chose to come back after a short time so that their relatives would not miss them. They built a grass house facing east. They said that anyone who died could come to the medicine house and return to life."

Whispers came from every direction. Anthony jumped as disembodied voices spoke in his ears in languages he didn't know.

Another shadow appeared on a nearby stone. A man ran swiftly from one end to the other. A feather brushed Anthony's cheek as an arrow flew past, striking the shadow on the stone. The man fell, dead.

"When the first man died, the people gathered in the medicine house, singing and praying for the man's spirit to come to them."

Wind whipped the fire into a tall spire until the heat caused sweat to break out all over Anthony's body.

"On the tenth day, a whirlwind blew in from the west, came around to the east and entered the medicine house. The whirlwind vanished, and in its place stood the young man."

The fire died down revealing a young man in native regalia sitting where the old man had been. Anthony thought he was seeing things and rubbed his eyes. Grandfather's voice came from just behind him.

"The people were happy, but I was angry. They had not followed the rules I made."

Anthony spun, standing up, but there was no one behind him. He spun back around, and Grandfather was sitting as if he'd never left his spot. The old man leaned forward, the firelight casting terrifying shadows over his face.

"The next time someone died, I got to the medicine house first and sat by the door. The people prayed and sang, but when the whirlwind came, I slammed the door. From that day forward, death lasted forever."

The fire died down to coals. The shadows stretched in every direction, and the old man became a silhouette against the horizon.

"Do you get it kid?" the old man asked, his lips moving for the first time. "Do you see how this story relates to you?"

Anthony gulped. He wanted to nod, he wanted this to be over, but he was sure Grandfather would know he was lying. "No sir. How?"

The old man leapt across the fire pit, inches from Anthony's face before he could react. Beneath that wide-brimmed hat were the eyes and snout of a coyote, its lips curled to reveal dangerous teeth. Its breath was hot and rancid against Anthony's face.

"Because your brother is going to get me to the moon, and if you don't help him, it will be the whirlwind for you and your whole family. ¿*Entiendes*?"

Anthony woke to banging from outside. Max was already working on the rocket. He jumped up to rush outside, to join his brother, but his mother caught him in the doorway.

"It is Monday, *m'ijo*. You have school today. Go get dressed."

The dream was fading, and with it some of the urgency, but Anthony had never been less interested in school. And just as he resigned himself to his fate, Aunt Ari came in, holding two cans of paint and a handful of brushes. Just as she promised.

Anthony looked longingly at the rocket. It wasn't fair that Max would get to work on it alone. What if he screwed it up? Uncle Chencho would be away too, working, but promised to staple the wires to the inside of the rocket when he got home.

"Don't worry," Max said. "I know what to do, and I can work on it until you get home."

If they waited until Anthony returned to paint the rocket, it would still be wet that night, and the Commies might get to the moon first. Besides, there was a pair of yellow, ravenous eyes in the back of his mind just waiting for him to slow down.

"Okay, Max," Anthony relented. "You can paint it."

He spent his school day thinking about the rocket and Max's good luck charm. If Max put his necklace in there, that made it his rocket, didn't it? Unless Anthony had one too, which he didn't.

Then Bisa's story about the condor feather came back to him. The Condor would make a great name for the rocket, and naming the rocket trumped good luck charms as far as ownership went. Heck, he could even use the condor feather as a stencil, and it would be his good luck charm.

The paint was dry by the time Anthony got home, and the rocket looked just like it did in Anthony's drawing. There was even a little porthole so the pilot could see outside. He fixed a few unpainted areas where Max got sloppy or couldn't reach, then he ran inside and came back out with the feather and a small paintbrush.

Max watched as Anthony wrote, sounding out the letters as he went. Then Anthony painted over the edges of the feather in black paint. The feather stuck, but Anthony liked it and decided to leave it that way.

Chencho could just barely fit his upper body into the rocket as he stapled black, white, and red wires. Following Anthony's direction, they ran from the hatch at the bottom up to the control panel, attaching to two switches and one big button.

When Chencho crawled out of the capsule, Max stood there with his necklace in his hands. "Here, Uncle Chencho. This needs to hang above the controls."

Their uncle gave him an appraising look. "You sure about that, Maxy?"

"Yeah, I'm sure. It's for good luck. We're gonna need luck if we're gonna beat the Commies."

With a chuckle, Chencho took the necklace and stapled it to the ceiling above the control panel. The little silver coyote head swung forward and back, glinting in the light from the port hole.

The three of them stood back and looked it over.

"I think it's done. You going to launch it now?" Chencho asked.

"That's silly," Max said. "We have to wait until the moon is up."

That evening, after dinner, everything was ready. Anthony pulled a chair away from the dining table and stood on it.

"Attention! The temperature is a mild seventy degrees and the weather is clear tonight in Cape Cicaro. Perfect conditions for a launch."

Grandpa, Bisa, Mama, Ari, and Nani gathered around and clapped. Max opened the screen door and Anthony led the group outside where Papi and Uncle Chencho waited to close the rocket's hatch.

He was proud of what he and Max had made. They'd done almost the entire thing by themselves, and Max never even complained about the work. The rocket was shiny and red and all the little nails looked like rivets. The nose cone was smooth and the tail fins looked just like in the movies. Three cylinders of air duct were taped to the hatch that Papi held, painted black to be the engines.

Anthony wished they had time to make papier-mâché helmets, but it was more important to launch tonight. He waved to the crowd, and climbed inside the rocket. Max copied his moves exactly, and Papi re-attached the hatch.

"Check engine," Anthony called from inside the rocket.

"Check!" Max echoed.

Anthony looked out the little porthole. Everyone was lined up and smiling. Mama clapped, her cheeks glowing with pride.

"Oxygen at full?" Anthony asked.

"Check!" Max said.

"Ready for ignition in ten."

"Is it supposed to do that?" she asked as her smile fell, though it wasn't clear what she was talking about.

Anthony pressed his face against the port hole. "You guys are supposed to count down!"

First grandpa, then Bisa, Nani, and Papi started counting backward. "Ten, nine, eight…" Wisps of smoke passed by the porthole. Anthony searched for the source, but the smoke looked like it was coming from their engines. Which was impossible.

The rocket shook back and forth as Max rocked within the small confines making exhaust noises.

Grandpa and Nani kept counting down, though everyone else had stopped. "Seven, six…"

The smoke was thick enough to obscure his view entirely.

"Are you two okay in there?" Papi asked.

"Yeah, we're okay," Max said.

Mama sounded panicked as she said, "Something's burning, Diego! Get them out of there!"

Papi ripped the hatch off the rocket and Chencho pulled out a flailing Max.

"No! We have to go to the moon!" Max yelled as he beat at Chencho's shoulders. Anthony followed him out, frowning.

"Why is everybody so—" He broke off when he saw smoke jetting from the tin engines taped to the plywood hatch in Papi's hands.

His grandparents' eyes were oddly glazed as they continued the countdown. "Three, two, one, blast off!"

Fire shot from the engines, burning through Papi's shirt before the hatch blasted out of his hands. It flipped chaotically, shooting off in random directions, then it came straight for the gathered family. Everyone leapt out of the way, and the hatch hit the ground, the engines doing their very best to tunnel into the earth.

Anthony pushed himself up off the ground, coming level with the porthole they'd cut into the rocket. A pair of hungry eyes stared back at him. *"If you don't help him, it will be the whirlwind for you."*

"Get the hose, Diego! Put the fire out!" Mama yelled.

"No!" Anthony screamed, the whole of his dream coming back to him. He ran to the hatch, grabbing it by the edges. He couldn't lift it, but he slid it closer to the rocket, the heat of the jets searing his face, the roar of the engines filling his ears. Mama screamed silently at him to get away from it, but he ignored her. Finally, he pushed the hatch next to the rocket, but Anthony couldn't pry it off the ground.

He looked around at the others standing motionless around him. "Help me!"

Max was there first, for what good he could do. Uncle Chencho guided him away. "Let me try!"

Papi did the same for Anthony despite the weeping burns covering his chest and arms.

The two of them got a few fingers under it, then pried against the force of the jets. Slowly it rose until it stood on end, facing the body of the rocket. It shot out of their grip, slamming into the rocket, jetting the whole thing into the street. It left a plume of smoke across two city blocks before it ricocheted off the curb and shot skyward.

Anthony hadn't noticed them at the time, but neighbors had come out to see the source of all the smoke and yelling, and now the entire community stood in their lawns, watching their rocket disappear into the night sky.

Mama threw her arms around Anthony and Max, squeezing them wordlessly.

Bisa let out a deep sigh and shook her spoon at the sky. "Ay. Coyote, you old dog. You finally found a way to claim the moon for yourself."

Gaps in History

"Holy shit," Olivia muttered.

N.S.A. and F.B.I. Questions Family Over U.F.O.

She couldn't believe it. Something happened, something *huge*. The article detailed how the Russians were alarmed, asking questions regarding a launch early November 1957, only a month after Sputnik. A launch that happened on U.S. soil.

A launch three months before Explorer I.

Who? Olivia's mind raced as she checked dates on her phone. NASA wouldn't be formed until the following year, and would surely have announced a project of their own. Although San Cicaro had some plane factories left over from the war, it did not possess a real aerospace program and never had. *And if the government was looking into it, it means they did not know who sent something up.*

After reading the story, Olivia checked microfiche plates of other newspapers for similar dates. The *Cicaro Inquirer*'s November 6th edition, published a day after the *Observer*'s, was missing as well. Suspicious, Olivia logged onto the rival newspaper's account, and did a quick search. She found herself staring at a 404 error. The archive entry did not exist. The *Cicaro Inquirer* was incredibly meticulous, and it was unlike them to have a gap in their records.

Unable to let it go, she checked them all. *Washington Post. New York Times. San Francisco Chronicle. Los Angeles Times* and *The Wall Street Journal.* Each time, she found nothing.

Keep this between the two of us, will you? No reason to worry Marco, Olivia recalled Melissa's words. Words that had been sent through her personal email, rather than over work's servers.

Gulping, Olivia dragged and dropped the PDF file of the scanned newspaper and attached it to her reply.

Here you go. I don't know why this goofy UFO stuff interests you. I think you need to head to Nevada if you want Area 51, Mel! ;)

Sent, Olivia forced herself to focus on her work. Fifteen minutes worth of digital scanning later, and her phone buzzed. She jumped, wondering if it could be Mel. Or Keanu trying his luck again.

Taking a glance at the notification, she groaned. Animal Control Officer Carl Satrum. "Can't this guy take a hint?"

Shaking her head and ignoring the text, Olivia's eyes danced over the list one more time. A date stuck out to her. June 25th, 1965. Carl had mentioned that date once, something about the start of a major reform for the city pound. It was jumping ahead a little, but it helped to reclaim her focus.

Fetching the microfiche plate, she slipped it into the reader, and sighed with disappointment.

"Head of city pound to retire," she read aloud. "Why are you so interesting, Mr. Robert Griffin?"

Animal Control
J. Rohr

Every beach is the same, yet different. Inhaling the salty air, it reminded Chuck of a Florida shore. He could almost imagine himself still strolling the whitest beaches in the world, cruising outside the City of Five Flags. The place seemed like someone making one of his mother's specialties. Oh, they followed the recipe, but little differences corrupted the cuisine. Enough to make a familiar taste seem foreign. That oddity turning the whole meal into something unpalatable. He could only taste the difference. He wanted the familiar but knew he couldn't go back to it.

Unnourished by the wilderness of Morro Strand Beach, Chuck returned to his car. Starting the engine, the Oldsmobile grumbled to life again. The Super 88 Holiday hardtop growled mighty savage, though Chuck couldn't help thinking it reminded him of his dad dying of cancer. A certain choking groan to the sound. Not that he saw the old man towards the end. Told to stay away—Momma wailing, "You're the reason he's dying!"—Chuck had got in the car and found himself on the other side of the country before his blood cooled.

With no real route in mind, he had knifed through states until turning onto 66. Shunned by folks since the interstate arrived, Chuck liked the cracked pavement and dying towns he passed. Parts of the country left to starve out of existence, so a new era could shine. Feeling akin to Route 66, he had kicked up a fleeting grin on the road.

Driving up the West Coast, Chuck wondered why he expected to find comfort with his family. Never knew it as a child, so no wonder they offered barbs when he needed them most. He pressed the pedal down and left the past behind.

As he passed through Peach Springs, Arizona, another town on the way to ghosthood, he stopped at a diner. There he had seen a subterranean fuzzy duck cutting up old magazines.

"What's the story, morning glory?" he had asked.

She had given him a disdainful expression only teenagers could cast, hurled at those deemed too old to use the youthful tongue. He knew it well from his time as a teacher, so barely felt the jab. Ignoring it, Chuck hadn't notice her soften as she absorbed him with her eyes.

"Cut-up technique," she had replied. "Puttin' together my own word from the bird. Ya dig?"

"I like to think so."

The young beatnik then showed him a sheet of paper covered in clipped phrases. Reading it, he had the feeling she meant it to be poetry. Unfortunately, it was the same old howl he heard the last decade, an echo rather than anything fresh—"Sputnik spiraling through the supernatural darkness casting an eye on the jewel of California." One of her magazines, however, had captured his attention.

She had passed it with a wink and a smile, and Chuck perused the contents of Out West while he sipped hot mud. Browned and brittle, flecks of pages fell away as he turned up an article describing a place called San Cicaro.

Despite sections already snipped, it detailed a city that called to mind when life seemed a dashing, bold adventure. So, Chuck had figured on a fresh start in the land of sunshine.

Yet, he hadn't burnt rubber straight to San Cicaro. Instead, he had stopped in Morro Strand first, a place his father always meant to, but never would, get to visit.

Chuck took a final look over the sea. He wondered what would really be different there. Familiar yet alien, he could only hope the strange meant gold. He put the car in gear and headed for San Cicaro.

Chuck did his best to not eavesdrop. Still, bits of conversation slipped in his ear.

"Have you acquired anymore, uh, *lepus cornutus*?"

"No, but when we do, I'll call you."

"How soon might that be?"

"I'll call you when I call you."

"But..."

"*Jeoliga*."

"*Shénme*?"

"Beat it!"

Hearing approaching footsteps, Chuck did his best to appear absorbed by a pinup calendar. He appreciated the artsy tease of foamy soap hiding the bathing beauty's nipples—the clever use of foam more than the tits. Into the room came a burly man who trudged behind the desk Chuck sat in front of. The bear dropped into his chair like a sack of dirt, sighing the way miners do after emerging from the earth. Popping a coffin nail out of a deck of Luckies, he threaded a cigarette between his lips.

"Smoke?" he offered the pack to Chuck.

Chuck shook his head. The burly man opened a lighter. Across the chromed steel, Chuck noticed *MSgt* engraved above the name Robert Griffin. Below it, the etched image of a tank.

"What'd you drive master sergeant?" Chuck pointed at the lighter.

"M26," Robert snapped the lighter shut. "You in Korea too?"

"Tomahawks—23rd infantry."

Robert picked up a sheet of paper. Chuck recognized the form he filled out a day ago. Robert raised an eyebrow.

"Says here you've been teaching high school."

"Yes, sir," Chuck nodded. "Back in Florida, I taught math at Pensacola High."

He gritted his teeth. He took pride in his time as a teacher. So, he filled out the part about previous employment honestly, not realizing until now how it potentially opened him up to exposure. "Please, don't make this difficult," the vice principal had said, as Chuck was escorted out like some plague carrier. He still remembered that beady eyed crew cut looking at him the way people react to shit on their shoe.

"Now you wanna do animal control?" Robert said. "Seems like a step down."

"Depends on who you ask," Chuck said.

He mentioned hearing only good things from his current landlady. A raven-haired firecracker, she hooked him at a local gas station. After helping her fill a ten-gallon can, Chuck had found himself roped into mowing her lawn. Low on cash, he had accepted the job. Afterward, she mentioned having a spare room. In exchange for chores—weeding, painting the house, etc.—she'd forego rent until he found a job. Chuck said he didn't mind the offer, though he didn't know where to start looking for proper employment. That was when she pointed him towards animal control.

Robert chuckled.

"So, you're staying with Burro Flats Betty?"

"At her place," Chuck said. "I don't foresee anything romantic."

"Hey, I wouldn't judge," Robert smirked. "She looks good for sixty, I tell you what. My wife's thirty and don't look half as swell."

"I'm sure she's beautiful," Chuck said. "What it comes down to is, I need a job. Betty spoke highly of this one and so far, I've got no reason to doubt her."

Robert nodded. He rummaged through drawers then pulled out a blank form. Grabbing a pen, he filled in boxes as he chained cigarettes.

"She's good people," he said, mashing a butt in an ashtray. "If she sent ya, and you're an army guy, that's good enough for me."

Chuck felt the tension spill out of his spine. A knot melted and poured away, one he got so used to, he didn't notice until he felt the absence. At ease, he wondered if life might be getting brighter.

"I'm not even gonna waste time calling your old job," Robert said.

Chuck stiffened.

"Probably got caught with some Quentin quail?" Robert grinned. "Am I right?"

Chuck almost frowned. However, his starving wallet urged him to force a chuckle. Unable to afford disgust, he hastily recalled a gym teacher's jailbait jokes. Tossing a few tasteless tidbits seemed to relax Robert.

"Let's just say," Chuck added, "I didn't get along with the administration."

The view from Chuck's window showed the whole city stretching on. Sunset shadows shrouded San Cicaro but streetlights flickered to life, glittering. He felt as if the twinkling city invited him in from the outskirts, with bejeweled avenues casting a welcoming glow. People on the street drifted along aimlessly, their footsteps slowed by the summer heat.

He saw luminescent shapes take flight from a rooftop some ways off. For a minute he thought it must be fireflies, but the swarm seemed too large. However, he didn't know any kind of birds that glowed in the dark. Squinting, he lost sight as they flew away, becoming Christmas lights over the sea.

Glancing down, he saw a couple idling along the shore. He watched them join hands. Prince Charming in Bermuda shorts escorting his princess in a poodle skirt. Observing the couple, so casually openly romantic, he wanted to hurl a beer bottle at them. However, the one in his hand still contained suds. Tossing it would be a waste. Instead, he left the widow's walk.

Going back into his room, Chuck found Paul Anka's "Put Your Head on my Shoulder" spilling out of the radio. Crackling static made the song sound ancient. Sipping beer, he murmured along, swaying and dancing with himself.

A knock at the door interrupted. Frowning, Chuck went to answer it. Pulling the door open a crack, he saw his new landlady standing there.

"How can I help you?" he said, opening the door wider.

"You get that job I sent you for?" Betty asked.

"I did," Chuck said. "Starting tomorrow."

"Good. Then you tell that Rob Griffin we're even." She dusted her hands.

"What if he's not happy with me?" Chuck grinned.

"Then you and I are gonna have words."

She shook a finger at him then started away. Betty took her time as if nothing in the world could make her hurry. Chuck never knew anyone who seemed happy to go so slow.

Closing the door, he heard the radio choking on its own static. Nothing now except a sputter of intermittent clarity. He gave it a slap. When percussive maintenance failed, he turned it off. Standing in silence, he heard the sea lapping at the shore.

"This is my life now," Chuck said, standing in the room alone.

A howl pierced the stillness. Soon an echoing, unsettling sound replied. Both seemed canine, but the latter carried an almost industrial quality to it. Like something born of steel instead of meat. More important, it didn't sound very far away.

Despite a cold sweat inspired by the noise, Chuck crept back towards the widow's walk window. The baying made his bones feel rubbery, yet he felt a need to see the source.

He saw the couple from earlier running along the sand. They sprinted to a car parked by the roadside, diving in like infantry under fire. Soon the car rumbled to life and sped away. Chuck looked up and down the beach. Spotting a massive black dog, he nodded.

"Must be wild dogs around here," he murmured.

The black hound howled. The sound sliced through him like a knife. Chuck dropped his beer. The bottle fell, shattering on rocks below. The black dog snapped its attention in Chuck's direction. They locked eyes for a moment. Chuck figured the remains of sunset gave the animal its red gaze—burning coals which gradually turned away to scan the city. Chuck gasped sharply, unaware he held his breath until the dog looked away.

Retreating to his room, Chuck shut the place up tight. He pricked an ear, waiting to hear the howling again. A knock at the bedroom door caused him to jump.

"You got a minute?" Betty shouted through the door.

Sighing, Chuck shook his head to scatter the spiders weaving a fog in his head. He went over and opened up.

"Yes?" he said.

"I heard glass breakin' outside," Betty said. "You throwin' bottles around?"

"No," Chuck said. "I—it was an accident. I'll clean it up."

The howling sounded again. Betty frowned.

"Now's not a good time," she replied. "First thing in the morning, you get it before work."

"I can get it now," Chuck said.

"I said in the morning," Betty cast a dismissive wave. "My house, my rules."

That familiar phrasing opened a paper cut on an old wound. Nothing deep enough to draw blood, but the sting turned his mind back. His parents often used those words as the last hammer blow, sealing the coffin on any contention. He once thought they used it to avoid explanations they didn't have, though as he got older Chuck realized the reasons for some rules can be unsettling enough.

"Yes ma'am," he replied, figuring best to let the matter drop.

Chuck half closed the door as she moved away. He thought he heard Betty say, "Not gonna let him get eat before he pays me a dime."

However, she disappeared down the stairs before he could be sure of anything.

On his first day, Robert sent Chuck out with an animal control officer named Nick. They got into a white truck decorated with an animal control insignia. Nick behind the wheel, Chuck rode shotgun. He never met anyone who talked as much.

From the moment he said hello, Nick babbled like a brook. A veritable stream of consciousness, he poured out endlessly. Opinions on baseball, the weather, women, music, television, and politics.

"L.A. losing the Angels was selling the cow to buy milk. We don't need the Dodgers bringing their Brooklyn stink around here. Angels snagged twelve pennants and the last not too long ago in '56."

"I don't really follow…"

"Speakin' of following, I was watching *Have Gun – Will Travel*. Great episode. Paladin knocked these guys around. It reminded me when the Angels and Stars brawled back in '53. We need more tough guys like that, ya know?"

"I…"

"Like I heard the vice president is gonna run for governor of California. I might vote for him. You know Nixon, right? Remember when that mob tried to stone him in South America? Throwing rocks at an American, and he stared 'em down. That's what we need nowadays."

Chuck barely ever got a word in edgewise.

"You like meatballs?" Nick added, carrying on before Chuck even answered. "My Aunt's got this Swedish recipe that'll blow your socks off. Bah-boom! Blow 'em away."

Strangely enough, Nick's chatter provided a strange kind of peace. Although Nick never stopped talking, Chuck never needed to say anything. He learned to mostly just nod or toss out a quick word.

"You know Audrey Hepburn?" Nick asked.

"Yeah."

"Oh, man. I'd split her like wet pine, ya catch my drift."

"Yep."

"You too, right? I mean, who wouldn't? That's why there's two guys fighting over her in *Sabrina*. You see that movie? William Holden was in it. I tell ya, if I was him…"

Hidden in the silence, Chuck waited for Nick to talk about the job. However, he seldom mentioned work. As such, Chuck found himself learning things on the fly.

Patrolling public areas for strays, Nick talked about Ted Williams's batting average. Scraping roadkill off a street, Nick shared his reasons why *Playboy* Playmate Mara Corday outranked Pat Sheehan. Returning lost pets, Nick expounded on his philosophy regarding music—"It's good when it sounds good which isn't as simple as it sounds."

Then a call came over the radio that turned off the faucet. Chuck didn't understand all the codes yet, though he did recognize the grim expression taking over Nick's face. It reminded him of soldiers about to fire back.

"10-4," Nick said.

He snapped off the radio. For over a minute they drove in silence.

"What's the job?" Chuck asked.

"Garbage people," Nick shook his head.

He said nothing more. The silence made Chuck nervous. They drove through the touristy part of town into a stretch of shotgun houses. Ramshackle wood-frame mushrooms growing in the shadow of the industrial area. Parking behind a rust speckled, grey pickup truck, Nick stopped in front of a crooked house. A gabled overhang sagged as if waiting for an excuse to collapse.

Nick got out of the truck. Chuck hurried to follow him. Meanwhile, Nick stormed across the short front yard to a wooden gate. The closer they got the more Chuck could hear the faint whimper of a dog. The loud th-whack of a leather strap sounded. The whimpering stopped. Moving a tick quicker, Nick opened the gate and threw it wide.

The backyard consisted of dirt and a few sparse sprouts of unhealthy grass. Various junk littered the ground. Chuck heard men laughing and the clinking of bottles. A few feet ahead, Nick sped around the side of the house first.

"Aw hell," a male voice said. "Not you again. Did that noisy ol' bitch call you?"

"No, Morris," Nick said. "I just know if I pop by, now and again, you'll be doing the same dumb shit."

Coming around the house, Chuck saw a group of men idling on a porch. Greasy with sweat, they dripped the same as their beer bottles. One potbellied fellow in a rocking chair glared at Nick. Nearby, skin and bones in the shape of a dog lay on the ground. The animal was bound to a railroad spike by a heavy chain around its neck that was too short.

Carried by the wind, a faint smell of blood called Chuck's attention to a shallow pit on the far side of the backyard. He noticed bones scattered around it, possibly animal. Several resembled rabbit skulls but with antlers.

"Morris, what the hell are you even doing to that dog?" Nick asked.

"Can't you figure it out?" the man in the rocking chair sneered.

"Would if I could," Nick said. "But it just seems like idiots watching a dog die."

"We're trainin' him," a towheaded greaser chimed in. "When he pulls out the stake, he can eat."

"That's right," Morris said. "Nothing wrong with making a dog stronger."

"That dog doesn't look too strong," Chuck said.

Morris narrowed his gaze. The rocking chair creaked as he leaned forward.

"Didn't you hear me?" Morris said. "We're *making* it strong."

"Oh well," Nick threw up his hands. "Our mistake. The dog is just tired from exercise. It's not about to die of exhaustion or anything."

"So, what if it does?" Morris spit in the dirt. "Then we'll know it was too weak for Luk-Tin's boy."

"He's got a goddamn foo dog for Christ sake," Nick shook his head. "You know what? I'm not even going to bother. Get the dog."

He motioned at Chuck to move forward. Chuck hesitated. He counted at least six men on the porch. Meanwhile, Morris popped to his feet.

"That's my dog," he shouted. "I paid good money for it."

Nick turned to Chuck.

"Get. The dog."

Nodding, Chuck stepped forward. He kept an eye on the men along the porch. They glared at him. The towheaded greaser flopped a leather strop over his shoulder. Yet none made any real move to stop him.

Slowly getting on one knee, Chuck reached for the dog. It whined softly and tried to retreat, but the chain kept it from going anywhere.

"Easy," Chuck said. "I'm not going to hurt you."

Gently, he petted the animal. Each stroke made it shiver. He unfastened the chain.

"Pete," Morris said.

A stocky guy stepped off the porch. He pounded his palm menacingly. Chuck stood up.

"Hey buddy," Chuck held up his hands. "We don't need to…"

The thug punched him in the face.

For a moment, Chuck lost track of everything. The world became an unrecognizable thing he felt entirely detached from. He floated through it like a storm. Chuck thought he heard shouting, the way men do at a boxing match, a general clamor encouraging violence. The shattering of glass and a blurry glimpse of Nick dancing between a barrage of bottles. Then everything grew silent as Chuck's hands began to hurt.

When the world became still again, Chuck slowly grew aware of things. Like his bloody knuckles and the unconscious goon at his feet.

Breathing heavily, he glanced at the porch. The greaser flinched back a step. Chuck turned towards the dog. Even without the chain on, the animal seemed too afraid to move. So, Chuck scooped the animal up in his arms. He carried it out of the backyard, back to the animal control truck. Holding the dog tighter with each step, he whispered, "Everything's going to be alright."

"Don't ever let anybody tell ya Chuck's a fairy," Nick said. "This one's got hammer hands. I seen boxers that're sissies in comparison. A regular Rocky Marciano!"

Nick gave Chuck several slaps on the back. Chuck managed a crooked grin.

"I just worry about the cops," Chuck said.

"Eh," Robert waved as if clearing a stink from the air. "Cops don't care about those assholes. Plus."

He reached into a desk drawer. When he produced a bottle of tequila, Nick clapped and rubbed his hands together.

"Being a city employee," Robert said. "Has certain perks."

He held up the bottle. The label read "S.C.T. Especial de Bruja."

"San Cicaro Tequila," Nick said getting coffee mugs. "You can only get it here."

"Eighty bucks a bottle," Robert said opening it. "But I get one a year as a, shall we say, thank you."

Pouring a round he went on about the history of the booze. Originating during Prohibition, local legend claimed a bruja originally from Tijuana brewed it. First in a basement then, after the 18th got repealed, she opened a secret cellar somewhere in the city. A vanishing breed of tequila, every year the supplies got more limited. While some suspected a marketing gimmick, others believed the secret ingredient, found only in San Cicaro, might be disappearing.

"Drink this," Robert said. "You'll feel like gold."

He held up a chipped mug. Nick offered a toast to Chuck's first day. Robert cut him off the second it ran too long. "You did good today. You're part of the team now. Salut."

They drank. The liquid ran down Chuck's throat like a sunset, warm but not burning. He soon felt like softened butter and the world seemed capable of sunshine.

Even on the drive home, lights glowed a little brighter. Stopping at a red, he saw a kid folding origami birds then putting them in little cages. The boy's mom or sister—she seemed somehow young and old—sold the cages to passing tourists. Some puppet trick made it look like the birds flew inside. Then honking horns called his attention to the green light. Chuck drove off, happy to have not figured out the secret of the birds. He preferred to believe the paper flappers really took flight.

Eventually, Chuck got the hang of things at work. Within two weeks, Robert let him go out on his own. After a month, he found himself floating through most days. Oddly enough, he missed Nick's chatter. He didn't realize how much it distracted from his own thoughts until the silence reigned.

Patrolling for lost pets, he wondered about his students back in Pensacola. He almost wanted some to fail, at least keep struggling, as if they couldn't learn math without him. Scraping roadkill off a street, he daydreamed about his father's funeral. It must've happened by now. He imagined his sister explaining his absence while Mom keened, partly in mourning but also for attention. Some relatives probably speculated about him being a communist, fleeing the witch hunt headed by the Florida Legislative Investigation Committee. Although, he suspected they wouldn't call it a witch hunt. Wrapped up in such thoughts, Chuck almost didn't notice the nine tails on the fox carcass he binned.

"Ah, that's nothing. Haven't you ever been to a freakshow before? Nick said when shown the carcass. "Sometimes, they have stuffed critters with extra toes and limbs and stuff. Anyway, don't you worry Chuck. Lemme take care of disposal for you."

A month later, he fished a feline out of his net while wearing a thick leather glove. The striped critter smiled like a lunatic, but Chuck ignored the animal as he stuffed it in a cage.

"Lemme go!" a scratchy voice yawled.

Chuck looked around. He saw someone nearby waiting for a bus.

"You talking to me?" Chuck asked.

The person at the bus stop shook their head. Chuck glanced at the cat. The animal grinned even as it hissed. The sound almost like mad laughter. Shaking his head, Chuck got behind the wheel and kept on about the day.

Back at animal control, he went in the breakroom while Robert offloaded the caged strays. Pouring coffee, he overheard his boss say something about phoning Luk-Tin at the time. "We got a Cheshire."

Still unfamiliar with the local lingo, Chuck wondered what that meant. Since starting there he heard certain words, especially in the morning after a fellow named Otis arrived. He primarily worked the nightshift. Chuck once helped clean the truck Otis drove. Inside he found iridescent feathers, purple fur, and scales the size of a fist. When he mentioned the odd array, Nick simply shrugged.

"California critters," he said then changed the subject.

However, suspicions slowly grew in the months that followed. He got the feeling Robert ran some kind of side business selling certain animals. For instance, Chuck occasionally overheard his boss murmur, "*Daebak*," Korean for *awesome* or perhaps *jackpot*, whenever more exotic critters arrived. Robert usually then retreated to his office for hurried whispers over the phone. Afterwards, he sent everyone home early. Claiming a need to catch up on paperwork, the boss supposedly wanted peace and quiet. The next day cages would be empty.

That said, Chuck never made the mistake of asking about it. He preferred not to call attention to himself. Rather, he made note of the operation to better avoid stepping in its way.

Back in Florida he used to make waves. Here, he wanted to be left alone. That's why instead of going for beers with the other guys after work, he returned to the emptiness of Burro Flats Betty's. She kept saying other guests would arrive in the right season. No reason to doubt her, Chuck prayed that season took a decade to arrive. He liked the silence of her vacant boarding house.

Some nights he heard nothing except the shoosh of the sea. On such quiet occasions, he stood on the widow's walk watching San Cicaro glitter. The night never snuffed its sparkle. Some section of the city always glowed. In the morning, when anger and regret hounded him awake, Chuck looked out on the city. He almost felt invited, called to those places where the lights never went out. Yet, he stayed in his room, reflecting on the secret history of his life. Clandestine kisses, coded conversations, and the fear of it all.

Other nights, he heard the dogs howling. He watched the black hound walk the beach. The gold glow from San Cicaro and silvery streams of the Gatsby Rock lighthouse allowed Chuck to see the black dog prowling. In that strange mix of illumination, it seemed an ethereal animal. Flashing wholly into view, then nothing more than a gold tinted shadow in motion. Sometimes its red eyes drifted his way, and Chuck found himself less and less afraid of its stare.

"What do you mean?" Robert said.

"Nothing," Chuck shrugged while punching in. "I just think we should patrol those beaches because of the wild dogs."

"You seen dogs by the beach?" Robert asked.

"Yeah, well, a dog. Big black son of a bitch with red eyes. Is that an infection or something?"

"Where abouts did you see it?" Robert asked.

"Out by Betty's."

"Alright, I'll get Otis on it."

Two nights later, Chuck lay in bed listening to the howling. Suddenly the baying turned into barking. Chuck sat up. Even the black dog's unearthly sound soothed him from time to time. It made him long for an angry kind of music. But this made his blood cold. Between the barking, Chuck distinctly heard someone screaming in pain and terror.

Worry twisted a nauseating knot in his stomach. Even when silence resumed, Chuck sat on the bed frozen. He tried not to guess what it all meant, but a part of him knew. Still, he avoided such thoughts until he got to work the next morning.

"Oh, hey man, ya not gonna believe this," Nick all but jumped Chuck as he came into work. "Some goddamn dog ripped Amos to pieces last night. He was down on the beach, not far from where you're staying. Now he's in Lucia Bella. I mean, what's left of him anyway."

"But he's alive?" Chuck said.

"Barely," Nick said. "He wasn't alone—thank Christ—but the guy he was with lost a hand. Lemme tell you, my uncle lost his hand. He was a machinist and a boozer, so it was only a matter of time, but if he's any indication, it is not fun. He told me…"

"Yo, Chuck," Robert called from his office. "Can you come here a minute?"

The knot tightened. Chuck felt ready to vomit. Swallowing hard, he went into Robert's office. He sat down across from the boss expecting bad news.

Robert sighed, exhaling a dark cloud of smoke.

"You heard about Otis?" he asked.

Chuck nodded, "I can't help feeling responsible."

"You and me both," Robert said. "Hell, I'm the one who left orders but what are you gonna do?"

He leaned back in his chair. An odd familiarity crept over Chuck. He recalled similar conversations in Korea, especially in the aftermath of a bloodbath. He and Robert feeling like the cause of someone's suffering, yet secretly glad not to share it directly.

"I could take over his shift," Chuck said. "Someone's gotta do it anyway."

"Night shift can get a little rough," Robert said.

"Maybe that's why I want it."

"We'll see how you feel after a month," Robert replied, stubbing out his cigarette.

The next night passed rather pleasantly. Without daytime traffic clogging the streets, he cruised through San Cicaro casually. Every road flowed, more and more open as the night deepened. Sometimes a wind came sweeping through the empty avenues. It carried away the lingering stink of exhaust and left a salty ocean scent spiced by the bay laurels in the area.

Nick said the city liked to wake up in its makeup. So, the first few nights, Chuck mostly cleaned the roads. If dispatch directed, or he came across a carcass—shovel, scoop, into the bin. Not all looked like roadkill, something he could now discern, but Chuck paid little mind. Whatever left the unfinished meals, he didn't care so long as it left him alone. Granted, a half-eaten seal in a downtown alley seemed odd. Especially with the two-headed raven that plucked at the remains, which took flight as he approached. But Chuck accepted it by not really thinking about it. After all, no one paid him to explain the oddities. Delving into them risked rocking the boat, and these days, he preferred floating undisturbed.

On the third night, dispatch ordered him to a stretch of suburban road. They told him to drive until he heard croaking. Parking, Chuck got out of the truck. Shining a flashlight around, he couldn't see any toads though he heard them. That and a sound like someone shaking a leather jacket. Then a wet thud as if a sack of loose meat hit the truck.

Spinning around, Chuck spotted a toad on his hood. Instead of forelimbs, however, the animal owned greenish batwings. The sight inspired Chuck to aim his flashlight beam up.

Four or five winged toads bobbed in the light. Their tongues snapped insects out of the air. The sight caused Chuck to grimace. Yet, he got equipment out of the truck and netted two, causing others to fly off.

One tried to dive bomb him with a stinger on its rump. Chuck dodged out of the way. The winged toad hit the ground hard and bounced before flapping awkwardly into the air again.

Caging the fist-sized critters, Chuck wondered if these came from some other part of the world. He knew rhesus monkeys occupied areas of Florida. Brought over for a Tarzan movie, the animals got loose and now inhabited central parts of the state. In Korea he saw a lot of animals that seemed familiar yet different from what he knew.

Back at the boarding house, such nights made him wonder if he might not be as worldly as he once thought. His time in the military certainly gave him a perspective others lacked. However, as time went by, he missed the bliss of his youthful ignorance when the world seemed simpler.

Another night, a grizzled old man waved from the side of the road. He reminded Chuck of a Depression era photo he couldn't name. Something from Dorothea Lange. Like so many things, he knew the image, just not the title.

He parked and exited the truck.

"Where's Otis?" the man asked, dropping a cigarette in the gutter.

"He's in Lucia Bella," Chuck said. "I'm filling in for now."

"Well, I'll say a prayer," he said.

Chuck didn't know if he meant for Otis or him. Still, he followed as the fellow led the way to an apartment building.

"My own fault," he said. "I forgot to lock the basement door proper. They just let themselves in ya know."

He took Chuck around the side to a set of concrete steps. They descended into a dark entryway. Pointing down, the man waited for him to get going.

Donning his gloves, Chuck snapped on a flashlight. Heading towards the door, he noticed tiny five fingered handprints around the handle. Something clearly pawed at the door trying to get a grip. Similar prints on a trash can suggested it stood on the bin. If nothing else, Chuck liked the idea of the thing inside not being big.

Opening the entrance cautiously, he crept inside. Dust and spider webs coated the space. Finding a light switch, Chuck flipped on the overhead lamps. As they flickered to life, he caught something out of the corner of his eye. Turning towards it, he spotted a brown blur darting behind boxes.

Moving in that direction, Chuck followed more tiny prints along the tile. Holding his breath, he peered around a stack of boxes. Backed into the corner, he saw a bundle of fur peering up at him curiously. Breathing a sigh of relief, Chuck recognized it as a simple raccoon.

"Guess it's not always a freak show," he said.

Hands housed safely in leather gloves he reached for the animal. It hissed, but he kept on reaching. When the raccoon bit into the thick gauntlet, he grabbed hold. The animal gnawed on the leather but didn't come close to harming his hand. Eventually, he got it by the scruff.

Pulling the critter out of the corner, he stuffed the raccoon in a cage. He took it outside to show the man.

"Do you think there are anymore?" Chuck asked.

"Probably."

"I could set up traps."

"Maybe, but I want 'em out now before they attract those feathered snakes."

"The what now?"

The casual way people regarded crazy could make it seem ordinary. Chuck learned to follow the lead of people in San Cicaro. If they didn't seem spooked by an oddity, well, he did his best to act the same. Still, some days he returned to the boardinghouse unable to shake curiosity.

Then those howls hooked his attention. He went out on the widow's walk to listen. He heard a conversation between old friends. Sometimes he thought it might be lovers singing to one another. Other nights, he believed the dogs might be friendly enemies reminding one another best to stay on their side of town. It tempted him to howl himself, see what replied.

Most days, however, routine carried him along. It helped him not to think and the less Chuck thought, the more the world seemed to make sense. The night shift never felt like a winner's parade, but it rarely seemed like a mistake. Even the evenings he came back a bit bloody made him feel safe in the sense he conquered the night.

The call came in around midnight. Dispatch ordered Chuck to stop patrolling for coyotes and get over to a street on the west end of San Cicaro. Residents there complained about singing. Chuck figured they meant caterwauling felines. However, as he crept along the alley, he distinctly heard squeaky voices doing doo-wop. A tinny tenor started singing Jackie Wilson's "Lonely Teardrops."

Furrowing his brow, Chuck came around a dumpster expecting a pack of teens. Instead, he found several rabbits with antlers.

All his previous methods of rationalizing such sights failed in an instant. Something popped in his head causing him to stare agape as he realized there might be something more than weird about the animals in this town. However, he didn't get much chance to dwell on this realization.

Almost the instant he shined a flashlight on the group, the singing stopped. The rabbits flattened then scattered in several directions. A brown blur raced between his legs and Chuck felt an antler scratch the inside of his calf.

Jumping in pain, he tried to hop aside but only managed to trip over the bunny. Chuck fell hard on his side.

Hearing a snickering, he saw the rabbit sitting on its haunches, pointing at him with a paw. Chuck half rolled, half lunged and caught the animal by the antlers. As he got to his feet, the struggling bunny kicked furiously. Despite Chuck's heavy leather gloves, the long legs of the horned jackrabbit tore at his sleeve.

After caging the critter, Chuck got back in the driver's seat. Taking a deep breath, he got on the radio.

"This is Chuck," he said. "I think got a jackalope?"

"Yeah, they come out at night," dispatch said. "There's a fire not far from you. I need you to haul ass over there in case it attracts anything."

"10-4?"

Chuck started the truck. Instead of getting on the go, he sat for a moment. He could hear the jackalope crooning softly in the back of the truck. His brain refused to casually wrap the animal in the new normal. Chuck prayed the night wouldn't get any weirder.

Four weeks had passed, and Chuck lost his faith in prayer. The jackalope still haunted his thoughts. Perhaps it even distracted him.

Back at headquarters, Chuck jumped out and slammed the truck door. The tears down his side felt worse than they looked. The bleeding stopped a while ago, but the aches pained on relentless. He couldn't shake the impression of a jellyfish sting. Chuck let out a guttural bellow.

He barely saw what had grabbed him. The thing lunged out of the dark, slammed him into a wall effortlessly then vanished into the night. He chased rumors of a rose bush jellyfish whatsit all over town but got nothing.

When his shift ended, he returned to animal control feeling defeated. Bandaging his latest injuries, Chuck noticed the accumulated bruises and bite marks from the last few weeks. They used to make him feel like a conquer, someone who battled the night. Now, that sounded like the delusion of a chew toy.

He headed to Robert's office afterwards. Part of him wanted to quit. At the very least, he wanted some idea what stung him. Before he even got there though, the boss emerged applauding.

"I knew you could do it," Robert said. "Either that or run for the hills screaming."

"It's happened," Nick said, following him out. "We had this kid one time. He just about lost his damn mind. Then zip-zap-zoomed right out of town. I've seen slower lightning, but it sucks cuz he owed me five bucks from a poker game. I mean…"

"Anyhow," Robert said lighting a cigarette. "You've made it well past the point most folks usually quit."

"Yay," Chuck sighed. "I guess I win more weird, huh?"

"Tell ya what," Robert said. "It's been a rough month. Rougher than it's been in a long while. Take tomorrow off. If you want to go back on the day shift, quit, whatever—I'll understand."

"He ain't gonna quit," Nick said. "Chuck's not some limp wristed yellow chicken shit. Right buddy?"

Nicked slapped Chuck on the back. Forcing a smile, Chuck nodded. He thanked Robert for the time to think then punched out while Nick babbled on about the Legend of the Octopus born at the 1952 Stanley Cup.

"Of course, that was back when I lived in Detroit," Nick went on. "Honestly, I don't think anyone's born in California. We all drift here where we're meant to be. At least…"

"Hey, Nick," Chuck said. "I'm leaving."

Nodding sheepishly, Nick shut up. Waving goodbye, he turned and headed for Robert's office. On the way out, Chuck wondered, actually worried, what would happen to the animals he collected last night.

After a shower, Chuck laid down. However, unable to sleep, he went for a drive that turned into a walk along the pier. Throngs of tourists and idle folks with nothing to do killed the afternoon together in one slow flowing crowd. Strolling through them, Chuck made his way to the end of the pier.

"Excuse me," a light male voice said. "You wouldn't happen to be a friend of Dorothy's, would you?"

Chuck turned. A man in a light gray, three-piece suit stood nearby. He wore a fedora at a rakish angle and stood as if leaning into a conversation he could hop out of at any moment. Perhaps, if for some reason, he found it necessary to run.

"That depends," Chuck said. "Why're you asking?"

"Curious," the fellow said. "Hopeful? I've got a sixth sense for her friends."

"Is that so?"

"Someone once called it akin to radar, but in any event, I know where she likes to grab a drink, if you're so inclined."

Chuck took a final look over the sea, then nodded to the dapper man. That sounded just fine. "Lead the way."

Strolling along, the fellow introduced himself.

"George Gould but friends call me Gigi," he took something from his coat and offered it to Chuck. "I own a little paper shop here in town, Perfumed Paper."

Chuck accepted it, realizing it was a folded paper crane. He brought it to his nose and inhaled. A bouquet of fresh brine and seaweed filled his nostrils, and Chuck felt elated, like life itself blossomed in his chest again. "This is wonderful."

"Tourists love it. Nothing quite like writing to friends, with all the wish-you-were-here flair, giving that letter a little extra by having it smell like the beach."

"How do you get it to smell that way?"

"Trade secret." Gigi winked, pointing the way across the street.

As he stepped onto the road, Chuck grabbed his arm and pulled him back just as a rusty grey pickup roared by.

"That almost took my shoe off," Gigi shuddered. "Well, now I do have to buy you a drink."

"We should get that idiot to buy it," Chuck said. "They ran a red light."

He watched the pickup screech around a corner. The frame rattling like loose metal about to spill everywhere. Something about the blonde driver seemed familiar. However, a tap on the shoulder called his attention back to Gigi.

"Assuming we can't get them to," Gigi said. "I think we'll be fine on our own."

The man's warm smile and ginger beard reminded Chuck of quieter days. Thinking of cinnamon scented afternoons, picnicking along the beach, he smiled.

"You were leading the way," he said.

Gigi escorted him through a tangle of avenues to a twisting alley, where a hand-painted sign hung above a green door. It discreetly declared the joint Nancy's. Following Gigi inside, Chuck thought he heard the clatter of loose metal rumbling down the alley. However, as the door closed behind them, he left the world behind.

A dark corridor led the way to a bead curtain. The rain shower sound of the beads called all eyes to the entrance. Stepping through, Chuck felt himself being assessed. The presence of a stranger caused a noticeable tension to fill the room until Gigi appeared behind him. Chuck heard one or two soft sighs then a murmur of conversation returned.

Low lights gave the place a romantic quality, though Chuck understood they also allowed for discretion. Figures in booths lost their faces in the shadows. Just enough light to make one's way around the place.

Gigi took a seat at the bar and Chuck sat beside him. A lady behind the bar made her way over. She conjured thoughts of some migrant mother from the Depression. Those hardened by harsh times who still seemed soft enough to be kind because they knew compassion was the only thing keeping them human.

"Nancy," Gigi said. "I'd like you to meet Chuck."

"Pleasure," she said. "What'll you have?"

Chuck ordered a whiskey, and Gigi got a gimlet. While Nancy produced them, Chuck spotted a birdcage hanging over the cash register. In it, an origami bird fluttered about.

"How do those work?" Chuck said.

"Oh, you are new in town," Gigi said. "It's magic."

"You know what," Chuck said. "Before last night, I wouldn't've believed that."

"The shame is they don't last long. A few days at most then—poof—ordinary paper. Well, not entirely ordinary."

"Do you sell the paper?" Chuck asked. "Make it I mean."

"Yes," Gigi replied. "However, I can't divulge trade secrets."

"Not until I earn your confidences, eh?"

Nancy arrived with their drinks.

"To future lying about vows of passion, infinite and undying," Gigi paraphrased.

They clinked glasses and drank. The next hour vanished merrily. Gigi possessed a knack for breaking the ice as well as stirring things pleasantly. He simply started by talking about himself.

"My parents said I ended the Depression for them, but fortunately, I refused to peak with my birth."

Everything he mentioned, whether work or where he lived, offered an organic opportunity for Chuck to mention bits.

"It sounds like you've been everywhere," Chuck said.

"For a tick or two. I'd write a song about it if I didn't have a tin ear. Moved pianos for a while, but I never picked it up."

"Jumping from job to job sounds interesting. We could never afford to quit a paying gig."

"The trick is realizing they're all the same. People need something only you can give them."

"What if they can get it elsewhere?"

"You tell them they've been lied to which could still be the truth," Gigi winked.

Chucked laughed. As such, the two got to know one another without having to gruelingly mine for details. However, the ease of their connection almost took a grim turn.

Offered an outlet, Chuck poured. He didn't mean to but once the floodgates opened, he found it hard stop. Unable to find communists in Civil Rights organizations, the Florida Legislative Investigation Committee turned their attention on other communities.

"People they considered a threat to national security," Chuck rolled his eyes as he signaled for a whiskey refill. "Folks they could accuse of 'corrupting the youth.'"

It had only taken one accusation, probably from some pimple faced punk he failed. Soon the dominoes started falling. Everyone severed ties for fear of getting cut themselves. Guilt by association made him toxic in their eyes.

So much so even close friends wouldn't risk ruination sheltering a "lavender lad" pariah. Oh, they talked about wanting to, but they couldn't risk careers, families, reputations. Worse, they almost expected him to understand.

"As if you would do the same," Gigi said.

"One thing I learned in Korea," Chuck said. "Everyone is brave until they actually have to fight."

He waved a hand as if to dispel the dark clouds gathering. Taking the cue, Gigi shifted gears. The ginger paper wizard soon conjured a conversational trail that led them from the melancholy bog into the land of sunshine. There they joked and started stitching heart strings together. But time marched on, bringing almost inevitable demands of the day.

Gigi needed to get back to his paper shop.

"I've left my lovely assistant alone too long," he said. "Although, I don't mind squeezing as much work out of her as I can. She's leaving soon. Off to be a movie star. With any luck, her replacement, when I find them, will be good with numbers. The account ledgers insist upon it."

"Well, let me finish this real quick," Chuck raised a half full rocks glass. "And I'll walk you back."

"No, stay," Gigi said. "Enjoy your drink. However, perhaps you'll meet me tomorrow for dinner?"

Reaching into his suit coat, he produced a fragrant business card. Smelling like Italian cuisine, it simply bore an address.

"Riva Del Mare," Gigi said. "Best cioppino anywhere. Say, 8 o'clock?"

"It's a date," Chuck said.

Smiling, Gigi gave him a peck on the cheek as he hurried out. Chuck watched him go. For the first time in too long, a place—this city—started to feel like home. At the very least, somewhere he felt happy to be.

Finishing his drink, Chuck headed outside. Stepping into the alley, he pondered if he should stick with the night shift. His wallet seemed to have gotten fatter, which meant one less thing to worry about. As for the dangers, he'd certainly known worse. Yet he found himself wondering what it might be like working in a paper shop.

"About time," a gruff, unfortunately familiar voice said.

Chuck glanced over. He saw two men standing next to a grey pickup truck, and recognized Morris. Next to the driver side stood the towheaded greaser. It slowly dawned on Chuck they blocked the alley's nearest exit.

"You were in there a long while," Morris said. "Must've been having a real good time."

The greaser spit on the ground. Sneering, he shook his head.

"You got a problem?" Chuck said.

"Yeah," someone behind him said.

Chuck turned just in time to catch a sucker punch in the face. As another meaty hammer descended, Chuck recognized Pete, the goon he obliterated a while back. Blocking the punch, he brought his fists up. That's when the greaser joined the fray, and Chuck started to feel like a pinball bouncing around a brutal playfield. The world went out of focus then mercifully black. However, even in the dark, he half heard their conversation.

"Lemma stick him Morris."

"Put away that switchblade, you idiot. Pete, throw this fruit in the back of the truck."

"What's the plan?"

"We're gonna catch us a dog."

The cry of birds high overhead called Chuck back to the world. The shoosh of the sea tried to lull him asleep again. However, he was stirred awake by colors flashing by, flapping their way seaward. Sitting up, he found himself deposited in a shallow hole dug in the beach.

It reminded him of being in a foxhole, waiting for death to fall from above. Back then he did his best not to calculate the odds of survival, but the numbers rolled through his mind casually. Digits had turned into degrees of inevitability, every explosion had grown closer—the shiver of the earth changing the variables. Chuck had taken what comfort he could in the slimness of sums, before everything reduced to zero. A mortar shell had planted itself next to him, sticking out of the dirt like a grim sprout.

Suddenly, his entire life came into focus.

Oh yeah, everyone in high school had wanted to date Layla Ferlinghetti. Even the drama teacher Ms. Clarington ogled the buxom cutie's curves now and again. However, Chuck had realized he asked Layla out because she fit so obviously into an equation that he found hard to balance. Her presence beside him had acted as rebuttal against rumors inspired by implicative moments. Things like the way his stare used to linger in the men's locker room, or the possessive attitude he got about certain male friends, especially once they started dating girls. That time he once explained the difference between pink paints Mom chose for his sister's room. Or the day he had joined the football team in harassing an effeminate drama geek whose name he could never remember, though his face Chuck would never forget.

Each of these incidents were milestones constituting the sum of his life. Things he found comfortingly natural which everyone had mocked—"No son of mine gonna like that, goddammit!" It all formed a crooked line, yet one charting a definite trajectory.

While waiting for the mortar to explode, he had seen exactly who he was and how he wanted to live. Then it hadn't. And Chuck had decided to waste no more time on mathematical fallacies. He would never again apply the "correct" rule to an implicitly inaccurate assumption.

A terrible ache derailed the old calculator's train of thought. Chuck blinked, trying to clear his head, and looked up. The slack face of a dead jackalope stared down at him. Voices, not far off, spilled into the hole. Chuck recognized Morris and his men.

"How much longer?" the greaser whined.

"It's done when it's done," Morris said. "You just stay ready with that net."

"Black dog goes in the hole, we net it, and got the sonuvabitch."

"Right-o Pete. I guarantee that beast'll take down Luk-Tin's monster. No doubt."

"Maybe we oughta put another jackalope by the hole."

"There's one already. Let the wind do its job. That meat ain't cheap."

Considering his options, Chuck froze as a howl echoed along the beach.

"Showtime."

Staying low, Chuck peered over the top of the hole. He saw Morris and his boys in the flatbed of the pickup. Downwind, they stood ready to pounce. Another howl. Chuck turned in its direction. He saw red eyes bobbing along the night black beach. Then the silver stream from Gatsby Rock illuminated the massive hound. It looked big enough to take down a horse.

A plan popped into mind. Chuck calculated the odds and though terrible, he couldn't devise any other options. Grabbing the jackalope carcass, he sprang out of the hole. Running straight towards the pickup, he flung the dead animal at the three men. The bloody meat hit Morris square in the face. The greaser, however, hopped straight off. He flashed across the sand and tackled Chuck to the ground.

"Well now," he laughed. "Call me Barry Allen cuz—*oof!*"

Chuck thrust an elbow back into the goon's face and scrambled to his feet. Seeing Pete fast approaching, Chuck wasted no time demolishing the greaser. Two jabs and a right cross then he turned in time to duck under Pete's haymaker. Grabbing the thug around the waist, Chuck picked him up and slammed him into the sand.

A distinct *cha-chunk* sounded. Chuck saw Morris standing nearby pointing a shotgun at him.

"I wanted to hear you scream when that dog ate ya," Morris said. "But I'm fine with this."

Chuck braced, not for the blast, but for his chance to run. For he saw the red eyes coming up from behind, watched them turn into streaks. Another stream of silver spilled over the scene and the giant black hound of San Cicaro charged like a freight train.

Fangs flashing, it tore into Morris. It crushed him into the ground. The shotgun fired into the sand.

If nothing else, Korea taught Chuck not to think twice, especially when the red river ran. While Morris' goons stood dumbstruck, Chuck bolted to the pickup truck, leaping into the driver's seat. As luck would have it, he found the keys still in their slot. Starting the engine, he soon sped away.

The towheaded greaser shouted, begged him to come back. Bone-melting barks silenced the pleas then twisted them into blood curdling screams. As Chuck drove away, a howl echoed through the night. He never once looked in the rearview.

Finding the road, he aimed for Burro Flats Betty's.

The next day Chuck opened his eyes slowly. He didn't feel like moving, yet some survival instinct shifted him into gear. The machine needed to move to come back to life. Wasting away in bed only paved a route to rust and ruin. So, he headed into the morning routine.

Brushing his teeth, he noticed blood on his shirt. Flashes from last night stabbed into mind. When he got home, Chuck collapsed into bed. Not so much sleep as a lengthy blink, he jumped through the darkness to now.

Pulling off the shirt, he tossed it in the trash. He could wash off the stain, but not the memory. Better in the bin than lurking like a landmine in a dresser drawer. A reminder ready to blow him back into the nightmare.

Getting dressed, he started thinking about the dead jackalope staring down at him. He wondered if it might be the one that he had caught. Thinking about it, he could almost hear the little animal singing. It made him wonder how much of a difference stood between Morris and Robert. Some of the aching wounds from work tried to add their two cents, but Chuck couldn't blame an animal for doing what came naturally.

The people, however, they made choices.

That settled things for him. He drove to work, certain what needed to be done. His wallet protested, but some principles are worth more than silver.

"Sorry to lose you," Robert said. "If you change your mind, just lemme know."

"Thanks," Chuck said. He knew he wouldn't.

"What'll you do now?"

"I know someone with a paper shop," Chuck smirked. "I think I'll try that. See where it leads."

So, Chuck left animal control. Strolling the city streets, he felt on his way to a fresh, dashing, bold adventure. He looked forward to adding his sparkle to the jewel of California, San Cicaro.

Between Professionals

"Adamos?" Olivia read that line, then read it again. "Bartholomew Adamos?"

That couldn't be right. She knew that name from Carl's blabbering, and looked up the current Director of Animal Control. Sure enough it was the same guy, or at least it was. Last year, he stepped down after a major incident. Something about spraying bear mace into the eyes of an assailant. Carl had spoken at exhaustive length about regulations regarding the use of bear spray whilst on duty, which is why it stuck in her mind.

If it was him, he must be at least eighty or ninety. What is with San Cicaro and suspiciously youthful-looking elders?

Something in the water I guess...

The day was nearly over at last. The elevator car slid to a stop, and Olivia adjusted her bag as the door opened with a *crunch*. It felt good to be out of that basement, and she stretched her arms as she made her way past the library desk.

A whiteboard on the desk caught her eye however. "Discussion on freedom of the press and censorship in the Stanley Gray room, 4-5 PM."

"Talking about providence," she said, earning a stern "*Shhh!*" from the librarian.

Olivia stuck her tongue out at the librarian as the crone returned to her book, then started walking towards the hallway near the exit. The Stanley Gray room was not hard to find, and a voice could be heard from behind the cracked open door.

"… and while much of the events around the *Fairweather*'s sinking have been declassified, I know some journalists still in the business are trying to get more of the Office of Censorship documents released through FOIA requests. We'll be back next month with one of them to share more details. I know the French Film Society has this room booked after us, so if you have questions feel free to shoot me an email."

Olivia realized she recognized this man. Not in the flesh, but from photos on the walls of the *San Cicaro Observer* halls and offices. She found herself drifting towards the 70-some year old man gathering his things at the podium. "Excuse, are you Mr. Martin?"

The man flashed a smile that could warm the room. "Indeed, but please, call me Gil."

She smiled back, though shyly. "I'm Olivia Murphy. I think I started working for the *Observer* shortly after you left."

"A cub, huh?"

"Yes sir."

"*Gil*, please. I am definitely no sir. So what hot scoop have they got you on that takes you to the library, of all places?" He waggled his eyebrows. "Off the record, of course."

Olivia couldn't help but laugh. "Unfortunately, I'm on some mundane archiving task."

"Archiving?"

"Yep. The fire, back in the 90's?"

"Ohhhh," he scratched the back of his head. "Right. That."

The way he says that, I wonder if he had something to do with it, Olivia thought, but said nothing. "I did happen upon the news articles downstairs about the sinking of the USS *Fairweather*."

"Well then I should be asking *you* some questions! Join me for a beer?"

Olivia paused, reaching for her smartphone. It was 5:07 PM, plenty of time.

"It's not like Marco is going to check your messages until tomorrow morning," he offered.

"Oh, it's fine. I wanted to make sure we could get there in time for happy hour."

"That's what I like to hear!"

Once Gil had gathered his stuff, the reporter and ex-editor made their way out. Olivia waited until they were beyond the doors, and the stern disapproval of the librarian, before asking further questions. Before long, the pair were pounding pavement away from the library towards a more lively part of town.

"So did you ever find anything about the USS *Fairweather* while you were reporting for the *Observer*?" Olivia started.

"Not really. The closest I ever got was interviews with people who worked at that dock. But most of them were around 70 or 80, and their memories were shoddy. The way they spoke about it, you'd think it was a religious experience."

"So were they confused? Perhaps dementia?"

"Once maybe I might have thought so too, but spend enough time in this city and you'll learn the more obvious or literal answer isn't always correct. Occam's Razor is not so sharp in San Cicaro."

"Why? What other things have you seen?" Olivia asked as Gil turned a corner, leading her towards a little watering hole. The neon sign above called it "The Nu Bar."

"It'll take more than one happy hour to go through it all. You'll probably find there are things you'll come across in research that you can't always print. Sometimes you have to… massage some of the details to make the stories more palatable."

Massage or make stuff up? Olivia thought but dared not ask. Suddenly, Mel's outlandish and private request for the UFO article came to mind, but she chose not to ask that either. It would not do to burn any bridges. "Well then, anything you wish you could have told the full story about? *Off the record*, of course."

If you're drinking outside, seat yourself! Our staff will be with you shortly, was written on a blackboard beside the bar's door. Gil veered her towards a small round table with high chairs, paused when he discovered it was wobbly, and chose another that was more firm.

His silence disturbed Olivia, and she found herself wondering if he was perhaps offended by the question. Her chest squeezed with a smidge of anxiety as she looked at the paper menu, trying to decide on a beer with a low ABV.

It turned out, his hesitation was also fear.

"Yeah," Gil finally answered, ignoring the long pause between his answer and her question. "Every cop talks about having 'the one' case that sticks with them. Some reporters have that too, I guess…"

"We can leave it if you don't feel comfortable sharing," Olivia offered, hoping to flip his interest. The tenseness in her torso was already dissipating.

Gil opened his mouth to answer, then twisted his lips into a knowing smirk.

"You'll do just fine at the *Observer*," Gil trailed off with another pause, but cut back in, before Olivia was about to prompt him again. "But this is just between us. And be patient if it takes me a little time to tell it right. This one… it was more personal than most."

The Last Obituary for the Old Man

Vernon Miles

The Louis Bradshaw I knew didn't look much like an ecoterrorist.

In the years since then, I hear he's gone off the deep end. The wanted posters at the bottom of the FBI's Most Wanted lists show him with shoulder length dreadlocks and that Charlie Manson look in his eyes. The years had turned him into the wild, heathen caricature the J. Edgar bootlickers had wanted from the start. Maybe that had been their plan all along.

T.O.M. had that effect on people, I guess.

I couldn't contact Louis for an interview now, probably much to the dismay of the agents still tailing me. But the Louis Bradshaw I met in late 1969 wouldn't have looked out of place at a Young Republicans conference, apart from being Black.

Today, Louis is rumored to be somewhere in the Dominican Republic. The Louis I knew then hadn't been outside of New Orleans until basic training. After which, the 23rd Infantry took him away to Vietnam.

Outside of cryptic bits and pieces gathered here and there, his year in Southeast Asia is an enigma. Sometime in 1968, a troop transport brought him to sunny San Cicaro on his way home to New Orleans, but Louis never left the city. He kept the tight crew cut and the neatly folded clothes. Some of his comrades would tease him for calling police and authority figures "sir" or "ma'am." Yet beneath that façade, things had started to change for Louis.

I first drifted into Louis' orbit when I started becoming familiar with some of the faces in the College University of San Cicaro anti-war protests. As the only reporter at the *San Cicaro Observer* at peak-drafting age, I drew the short straw for the beat. After all, my colleagues were "the enemy" at these sorts of gatherings, or at least my hawkish editor.

A press badge is an appeal to humanity and a sense of law and order—in short, useless in the face of your average Bull Connor-mindset jackboot. I got in the habit of leaving it at home just to avoid the extra baggage. You travel light at protests. The basic kit consists of an average Nikon (we're the *Observer*, not *Life* magazine), a flask of gin, and a notebook with some firm binding in case folks get grabby. And maybe a bit of mescaline to add spice to the story.

Always bring a pen, but not because you'll use it. It's the sacrificial offering—you'll invariably take someone else's, and the cosmic balance demands you lose one there.

In this case, I was borrowing Lucy's. She'd been a friend of my first girlfriend at Berkeley. Although the relationship lasted only a few months, Lucy's friendship endured years longer.

Like Louis, she was a native of some nebulous corner of the vast American south until the youthful call to adventure had sent her rolling like tumbleweed into San Cicaro. But where Louis kept the caricature at bay as long as he could, Lucy had fallen head over heels for the aesthetic. Her beach blonde hair always slipped out from a loosely fitted black beret. Her long dark coat swept around her like some ancient nobleman's as she made her way through the crowd.

The protest was in full swing by the time I hit the campus. I'd walked the few blocks from our office and followed the chants echoing through the concrete canyons. Crowds had exceeded earlier estimates. Law enforcement tried to corral activity to the university, where any paperwork would be a problem for the campus police. But pockets of activists kept slipping through their barricades as though the police were kids trying to squeeze a water balloon.

My camera bounced on the strap around my neck as I pushed my way into the mob's currents, towards a more central position. Lucy had told me she'd be here with some friends, as if I had a clue what they'd look like. Square-jawed academics with horn-rimmed glasses marched alongside men and women who could have been mistaken for the Biblical disciples of Christ. I'd climbed on top of a red Plymouth Valiant foolishly left parked on the street. In my defense, I kept my steps confined to the boot marks already stamped on the hood.

From the vantage point I surveyed the scene, where individual faces blurred into the mass, over which flags and protest signs stood like banners. Finding her would be hopeless, and I made the best of it with a fast snap of the Nikon. Sighing, I stepped off the vehicle and steeled myself to question random passersby about whatever had them stoked. The war, whether the moon landing was real, and if Zodiac would take a working vacation to San Cicaro…

Before I could make a fool of myself, Lucy reached out of the sea and seized my elbow.

"Get your goddamn hands—" I started back instinctively before her familiar oval face cut the legs out from under my rage.

"You're a damn fool, Gil," Lucy scolded with motherly concern as she cut through the crowd, dragging me along. "Orange Hawaiian shirt with a white floral print? Cops will be able to track you across town for days in that."

I'd honestly thought the shirt would have been more fashionable among my peers. Maybe my tastes were influenced by too much time around my geriatric colleagues. "Well, my editor didn't think a square peg would fit this fox hole."

It wasn't that funny, but Lucy laughed at everything, and it was so genuine you'd feel guilty not joining in.

We rode a riptide across the street to her island of comrades. Seeing them now made me feel silly for thinking most of the crowd was alike. Lucy's friends were militant—the kind that gets called into a lineup with Weather Underground and the Black Panthers. Whatever other grey or brown nondescript clothing they wore underneath, all had the same black uniform jacket with a hand-stitched red tree on the breast pocket. Under it was the name "DRUIDS."

There were around ten of them. Ages ranged from a kid barely 17 to a woman nearing a graceful 70 by the looks of her. Some carried signs in their hands, either over their shoulders or leaning on them like walking sticks.

"No Development at Barlow Park" one said. The one next to it read "STOP APM."

I furrowed my brow at the second one, trying to imagine what federal agency they were upset with. Then I realized they meant Avalon Property Management, the company trying to build a new office building downtown.

I couldn't fight down the sharp burst of laughter as I read the signs, earning uniformed glares from the squad of black-clad militants. The older woman pursed her lips disapprovingly, an expression which made me think she and my mother might get along.

"Lucy, seems like the scale of your protest is a little…" I trailed off, gesturing back at signs demanding Nixon leave office.

Lucy's dimples faded as her smile dipped a little. She readied her arsenal of charm to diffuse the situation, but the older woman cut her off.

"What good is protest if you can't protect something sacred in your backyard?"

It's been years since all of this, so you'll forgive me for paraphrasing. Yet I'll never forget the way she said "sacred." I don't know that I've ever put as much belief or force into a single word as she had for that park.

The teenage boy next to her twisted his fingers tightly against the pole, knuckles going white with the exertion. He nodded with a sage agreement that belied his youth.

"It's a nice little area, for sure," I offered as a tactful appetizer. Although I wasn't sure I'd ever even been to Barlow Park. "You guys really dig this park, huh?"

It was a dumb question, a classic stalling tactic, but the woman and the others softened their glares a little. I scratched at my notepad with Lucy's borrowed pen like I had to write down some profound observation.

There are two kinds of reactions to a reporter writing something down: nervous concern or prideful validation. Your average citizen is usually going to opt into the former. That was doubly true a few years later after the Watergate story broke. The damaging potential of investigative journalism put every good American with skeletons in his closet on the defense. But these folks, the true believers, their postures straightened and they lifted their signs a little higher as I took notes.

"Sacred" was the only note I have from the campus that day. And in the margins "ask Lucy if she knows where to get blotter acid."

Not long after that, the police had enough free speech and started to close in on the students with billy clubs. Dutiful fox that I am, I started making for the hedges as soon as the dogs came barking. But Lucy, a veteran of dozens of protests, pulled me back into the group and gave the others marching orders.

"I'm getting Gil out of here," she said. "I'll meet you all back at Tom."

They dispersed and Lucy took me on a diagonal tack through the stampeding crowd. At the very least she saved my Nikon from being crushed by the herd. And likely a few of my teeth from the SCPD's boot-based dental surgery. We scampered down an alleyway to a side street in front of Missy's on 96th.

A black Lincoln Continental immediately slid up to the curb, and the driver reaching over the passenger seat to open the back door. I didn't have time to protest or question before Lucy ushered me inside, climbing in a second later. She barely slammed the door shut as the Continental's tires screeched to life and the boxy car bolted down the avenue.

"I told you we needed an evac point," the driver growled, a Black man with strikingly angular features and a tailored grey suit complete with tie. Strange attire for CUSC that year. A pin on his lapel depicted a blue shield with four white stars, sparkling with the light of a police car that zipped past.

"I never disagreed," Lucy fired back, but with the same gentle laugh that had the same effect on him as it did on me. His almond-colored eyes flicked from the road ahead to the rear view-mirror, inspecting me, and she answered before he could ask.

"Gil's a friend at the *Observer*," she said. "Don't worry, he's one of the good ones."

I tried not to blush from the praise. When that failed, I tried to convince myself that it wasn't because it was Lucy giving it. If she noticed, she didn't show it.

"Just speaking truth to power," I croaked, hoping my joking boast didn't sound too sincere.

"Gil, this is Louis," she said. I cleared my throat and tapped at my own lapel. Lucy shook her head at first then looked up to Louis and saw the 23rd Infantry pin that caught my eye. "Oh, don't worry, *he's* one of the good ones too."

Louis swerved the car to avoid a bleeding protestor who stumbled into the street.

"I saw your piece on housing prices downtown last week," Louis said. "Good piece."

It was, but it had been Gary's, not mine. I was too tired and high off Lucy's praise to correct him and thanked him all the same.

"Want me to drop you off at the *Observer*'s office?"

Lucy started to confirm, but I shook my head and showed her my notebook.

"I don't have enough here for a story yet," I said, trying to subtly tap at the note that asked where I could score some acid. "Maybe if I could learn a little bit more about what you guys were hoping to accomplish... the Druids, right?"

Lucy tucked a few strands of hair back behind her ear and leaned towards the driver's seat.

"We should take him to talk to Tom," she said to Louis.

"Tom?" I tried to cut in. Louis eyed me uncertainly again in the mirror.

"Lucy..." he started.

"We're not getting anywhere the way it's going now," she said. "We need something big. Something that will get people's attention and stop the development."

If anyone else had asked, I'm sure Louis would have said no, it's too dangerous. Maybe that would have been better for everyone involved in the end. Then again, I've never met anyone who could say no to Lucy.

Barlow Park was a few blocks away, just far enough for me to build up expectations. By the time we turned onto 45th street, I'd expected a full redwood forest to have sprung up in the heart of San Cicaro. My heart dropped a few inches in my chest as the park came into view.

It couldn't have been more than a quarter of the block, barely more than a drug store in scale. Any hope I had of writing about a hidden utopia with a beloved playground or hanging gardens were dashed. The closest thing to a bench was a bus stop across the street. Most of the grass, the barest function of a park, was dried up and sickly.

The sole vestige of any ecological value was a sprawling oak at the heart of the park. One that also looked to be a terminal case. Spindly branches arched skyward like the withered fingers of some crone beseeching her pagan god. The trunk of the tree was swollen with knotted tumors that looked liable to burst and flood the neighborhood with puss.

As far as parks went, there'd never been a better poster child for redevelopment.

"Fuck," I whispered under my breath.

Lucy perked up with the same sort of validation her comrades had expressed when I noted their love of the park. But my meaning hadn't been lost on Louis.

"I know how it looks," he said. "But… just wait until you talk to Tom."

Given the status of the park, I'd started to suspect their mysterious guru was a street corner preacher. Or a new age philosopher who had access to some absolutely legendary pot.

I flipped the notebook closed and tucked it into my breast pocket as we pulled up. A handful of students wearing Druids' jackets were seated under the boughs of the tree on picnic blankets, with a perfectly bundled basket at each blanket. Despite their garb, the scene was more Hanna-Barbera than Hanoi.

We stayed in the car for a minute as Lucy and Louis talked through something that passed me by entirely. I was fixated on the leisurely scene, struggling to imagine where this was going to fit in my article. As they talked, more of the Druids I recognized from earlier started to show up.

Eventually, Lucy climbed out of the back of the car. Admittedly, I was tempted to ask Louis if the offer to drive me back to the office was still on the table. Finding out more about the Druids, particularly who this Tom was, became more of an objective for completion's sake than any journalistic quality. But I sighed and followed Lucy out.

I wasn't surprised when they hugged her. What caught me off guard was when the same elderly woman who'd scorned me at the protest gave me a grandmotherly hug.

"Well, I… okay—" I stammered as her arms wrapped around me.

"Tom said I was a bit too harsh on you earlier," she said. Her weathered cheek pressed against my chest before she pulled back and clasped her hands against my arms. "Thank you for coming out today."

Lucy had shed her jacket, and seemed to glide over towards the blanket closest to the tree. Louis already reclined there, pulling a halved sandwich from the box, offering me the other half. I was starving but declined. I didn't want to be any more in debt to people I knew would be disappointed by their role in my upcoming story.

"It's so peaceful here," Lucy purred. "The whole city just disappears into the background, doesn't it?"

The city very much hadn't. I keenly felt the attention of nearby pedestrians, not to mention office workers in the high-rises above. Worse, my orange Hawaiian shirt made me stand out against all the black jacketed students. I knelt on the blanket, trying to stay upwind of the basket to avoid further temptation.

"It's… yeah, it's nice," I said. "Is Tom swinging by today? Would it be possible to get a quote?"

Louis bit his lower lip as he considered the question.

"That's not really how the old man works," Louis said. "He'll tell you what you need to know, but it might not be quotable."

"Gil will find a way to put it in words," Lucy said, picking the crust away from the other half of Louis' sandwich. "It's why Tom sent me to find you."

That's when it clicked. Not Tom but The Old Man—T.O.M. There was a small knot in my stomach as I realized that Lucy hadn't sought me out on her own. After all, the Tate-LaBianca murders made headlines recently, the words "Ritual Killing" flashing before my eyes. And here I was, sought out by a group who called themselves "The Druids." I shifted uncomfortably on the blanket, wiggling her words back and forth in the crevice of my impatience and widening the gulf. Leaning back, I rested my hands on one of the tree roots running across the park.

"Is T.O.M.-The Old Man," I corrected myself, snapping the words off a little more harshly than I'd intended. "Is he coming or isn't he? If not, I need to get back to my office and file for the evening edition."

Something shifted in my hand, moving slightly like a python slithering along the jungle floor. I leapt to my feet, kicking over the basket in the process, my hands clung to my chest as I spun to look down.

But there was no snake visible in the thin patch of grass. Only the tree root.

"Lucy, what the fuck is going on here?"

Lucy stood as well and took my shielded hand. If it had been Louis or the older woman, I'd probably have run the whole way back to the office. Yet my legs froze in place and I let her take it.

"That's good," she said with a sincerity that almost made the whole situation seem less absurd. She tilted her head back towards the oak. "That means he wants to talk."

Sometimes when you're out in the world and reporting, you get caught up in the tide of a story and just coast along wherever it takes you. One of those pedestrians or office drones looking down might have seen this as one of those times.

It wasn't.

There was a profound wrongness to it, to everything, that I couldn't pin down. I'd always felt comfortable in cities, first in San Francisco then down here in San Cicaro, but suddenly I felt claustrophobic. Sweat started to drip across my brow and stain the pits of my floral shirt. I suddenly yearned for a time when this was all just open grassland and a brotherhood of trees near the coast. Those office buildings overhead started to lean in, threatening to collapse and swallow me, the Druids, our picnic baskets… and T.O.M.

With my mind lost to time and space, my feet fumbled. I fell toward the great obsidian behemoth at the rotten heart of the park. It's sweeping black arms kept the world outside at bay and encircled me protectively. And as I basked in the foreign memories, some little voice of myself wondered if the cure here might not be worse than the disease.

Lucy had stepped back then, away from my little bubble of reality, leaving me more or less alone with the tree.

Every part of my body trembled except my hand, which took all my concentration to hold steady as I touched the craggy surface of The Old Man. The Californian sun was surely the cause of its warm bark, but the throbbing pulse beneath was harder to rationalize. In the years to come, I'd tell myself I merely felt my own heart beating in that moment. Yet no explanation ever reached the same ring of truth as the realization of that T.O.M. was… something more.

Louis drove me back to the office in a cold silence. I kept my face pressed against the window, lazily watching the streetscape sweep past with a lingering revulsion I knew wasn't really mine. I barely said a word to my editors, slipping into my chair and plunking away at the typewriter.

Over the years, I've only told this story a handful of times, to a few people I was comfortable enough to share it with. I always added that I threw out a first draft, the version that told the whole story.

But this is a lie. Never once, while sitting at that desk, did I even consider telling the full story. Who would have believed me? It would have tanked any credibility I'd built.

It was cowardice. Every time I pass the office building on what had been Barlow Park, I drive or walk a little faster. I didn't just let T.O.M. die. I killed him, and something in this city will never let me forget it.

One of my photos from the riot was on the front page, but the story was three or four pages in. It was a few paragraphs, with a comment from the police and the CUSC student organizers. There was no mention of the Druids.

I didn't hear from Louis or Lucy for a few weeks after that. At first, I thought it was just because they didn't have more to say, or maybe they were busy. Weeks turned into a month, then two. My denial faded into recognition that Lucy and the others had been unhappy with how the story turned out.

Then in early January in 1970, Louis intercepted me outside the *Observer*'s offices. I tensed up and readied for the ex-G.I. to slug me, a tension that only slightly eased when he asked if I wanted to grab some coffee. He was quiet on the walk there, and preempting another uncomfortable silence I launched myself straight at the elephant in the room.

"I couldn't do it," I said, pausing as the waitress delivered the coffee as if to prove the point. "Even if they had published it, no one would have taken it seriously."

Louis raised his hands placatingly, signaling to my relief that he hadn't come to fight.

"Look, Gil, I get it," he said. "It was hard enough for me to believe the first time too, so I can imagine what you're going through."

I didn't answer, but the truth was that I hadn't reached the denial and rationalizing phase of my encounter with T.O.M. yet. It hadn't even occurred to me that what I'd experienced might have been some kind of hallucination. I liked the sound of that better than admitting that I believed in what happened and still excluded it.

"How… how did the others take it?" I asked.

"You mean Lucy?" Louis asked, cocking an eyebrow and sipping on his coffee. "She was a little disappointed, but give her time."

I don't know if he'd meant it to, but that answer was one of the more stinging responses. Furious I could handle, but the thought of letting the starry-eyed revolutionary down sank me a little lower into the booth.

"The demolition permit is pending, and we've got a petition in for a stay of execution, as it were, but it doesn't look good," Louis said. "Lucy's pretty distraught. We all are. There's a Planning Commission meeting to talk it over next month, but if that permit goes through before then…"

Barlow Park wasn't officially a city park and technically sat on undeveloped private property. Redevelopment would have been by-right without city intervention, and Louis and I both knew the city had very little incentive to drag their heels to accommodate—

"Wackos," Louis said, finishing my thought. "That's what they think we are."

"The matching costumes probably don't help," I admitted, and Louis snorted a small agreement. "Louis… why are you telling me this? I can't—"

"I know, I know," he said. He sat back and rested against the cracked leather cushions, looking up into the naked lightbulb hanging over the table.

For the first time since he'd approached me outside of the office, I really looked him over. Those big almond eyes were more sunken into his gaunt cheeks, and the pristine tie from earlier loosened below an undone top button. He was still more put-together than I was, but he clearly hadn't been getting any sort of meaningful sleep.

I waited for him to collect his thoughts.

"I guess I figured you're a part of this too," he said, still staring up into the bulb. "Maybe a small role, no offense, but you're in it too and you should know."

I saw him a few times after that, sometimes in the back of the Planning Commission chambers, and sometimes we'd meet for coffee. We developed a steady ritual. He'd ask what I knew about the city's development plans, I'd ask about Lucy. It was our little trade.

The Commission deferred on their decision for a few months, an act of bureaucratic handwashing from the Pontius Pilate School of Legislating. As expected, the demolition permit didn't wait half as long.

Without really intending too, I left work late one evening and wandered down 49th street until I stumbled on the park. It had been cordoned off with a roll of cheap plastic around wooden stakes, which struck me as an additional mockery of T.O.M. No dignified firing squad for The Old Man of Barlow Park.

The clawed arms of the tree were tucked in low, like a boxer shielding himself as he readied for a counterpunch. The sun was setting over the Pacific and elongated shadows danced across the sparse grass, the anxious ghosts of the city eagerly awaiting a new member of their tribe.

When I got to the foot of the tree, I tried to reach out, to graze my fingers once again along the surface of the bark. But an aura of unwelcoming left me unable to close the last few inches.

"Speaking truth to power," came a familiar voice from the street behind me. I whirled around to find Lucy standing there, carrying a bag in each hand from a nearby hardware store. "Isn't that how you described your work?"

I'd played this conversation out in my head a dozen times but all the rehearsed excuses died in my throat. Even silhouetted by the setting sun, I could see Lucy fighting back tears.

"And here I called you one of the good ones," she said. She set down one of the bags to run her sleeve across her cheek.

"The hell was I supposed to write, Lucy?" I shot back, deciding that acting indignant felt a hell of a lot better than feeling guilty. "Local advocacy organization takes its orders from a talking tree?"

"T.O.M. is more than that and you know it," Lucy said, a venom I'd never expected to hear from her slipping into the words. "You just had to write the truth."

How the *hell* was I supposed to convey the truth in mere words? Language alone could never have explained the sensation, the connection. Maybe if the *Observer* printed its papers in like, psychoactive ink, people might have felt it, have experienced it. But words alone were hollow imitations of a truth no one could otherwise have believed.

"No one would have listened," I answered. It felt pathetic even to my own ears. "No one would have even noticed."

"I would have," she said.

The sun sank a little lower, the orange Pacific horizon receding into a purple twilight, and neither of us moved.

"Goodbye, Gil."

I started working my way back towards the edge of the park as she started to resume her walk.

"Lucy, wait," I called out, jogging to catch up and narrowly missing a raised root. "What are you going to do?"

Lucy scoffed but didn't stop or turn around.

"We're not going to let them just kill T.O.M., that's for sure."

In her rush, she'd left one of the bags behind. I figured it would have made a decent hostage to force her to come back. So I grabbed the handle, and found the bag surprisingly heavy.

"Jesus, Lucy, what are you—"

Nails. Lots of nails, and what looked like some dynamite beneath.

Lucy realized her mistake just a few seconds after I did, and stormed back towards me. A handful of questions jammed up in my throat, but none escaped before Lucy snatched the bag away. When we were face-to-face I felt myself shrinking away from her unfiltered, spiteful rage. Looking back, I suspect that anger wasn't hers alone.

At the last moment, she let out a long sigh and her hardened features softened a little.

"Go home, Gil," she said. "I'll see you around sometime."

I just nodded. I was pretty sure by then we both knew we'd never see each other again. I watched her as she receded down the block until she turned the corner, never once looking back. I stepped over the low fence and started to trudge up the hill.

Whatever vestiges of sunset remaining had since vanished, leaving the tree a shadowy spire that swallowed the neon glow of the streets around it. The oak seemed impossibly far this time, warping my sense of distance as a defensive mechanism. But I wouldn't be deterred, and by the time I reached the trunk I think T.O.M. had recognized that.

The earlier aura of impenetrable foreboding was gone, as if the tree had resigned to bring me once again into confidence. My fingers slid over the bark, just as warm to the touch as I remembered.

As my fingers traced along the ancient grooves, slipping into surprisingly deep crevices, I felt a sudden sense of indignation. My concerns about credibility, professionalism, it all felt so… small. The Old Man was in a war for survival, not just for his own life but for the memory of what had been.

I tried to pull my hand away but found myself caught in place, pinned to the tree. I'd wanted this after all, so why not see it all. T.O.M. justified everything that would follow, for the sake of both his brother and himself. He and his followers had no choice. If they wouldn't listen to reason, then they'd—

I finally managed to pull my hand free and staggered away from the oak. The air had an unmistakable iron smell, and when I looked down to my hand it was coated in a thick red sap.

"T.O.M. has a brother?" I asked myself. Did Lucy know that?

I quickly dismissed the idea of contacting the police. Even if the notion hadn't been antithetical to everything I stood for, I would have a hard time dancing around the topic of the sentient tree.

For a few days afterwards, I tried reaching out to Lucy and the others, but they'd vacated their home shortly after my encounter with her. The only other information I could gather was that they'd gone a little further north to the outskirts of the city. But it was still a dead end.

I saw Louis one last time at a Parks and Recreation Commission meeting a couple weeks later. Avalon Property Management was promising to compensate for the loss of the oak by donating to a fund that would plant more trees somewhere else. Louis sat on the opposite side of the chambers from me. He'd lost his tie entirely and had a thick matting of black stubble growing on his angular cheeks.

He approached me afterwards and clasped my forearm in a firm, Boy Scout-style handshake.

"Makes sense that I'd spend my last day in San Cicaro in a city commission meeting," Louis said with a half-hearted chuckle.

"Finally headed back to New Orleans?"

Louis shook his head.

"Had some disagreements over the last few days with the others and a group outside Seattle needed some help, so…" Louis trailed off with a shrug.

There was more to it he wasn't telling me, though I probably should have guessed at it. I've wondered in the years since if he's grappled with whether he should have said more. Or maybe it just helps assuage my own guilt to imagine he's out there dealing with the same thing.

We wished each other good luck and left it at that.

By then there was less than a week to T.O.M.'s scheduled execution. I spent every day at my office waiting for some sign of what the Druids' next move would be. The answer came on a Friday afternoon when I was covering another, much smaller protest at the CUSC. I was hoping to see Lucy there, or see if they'd chained themselves to the tree like I'd once heard the older woman suggest.

I knew something was wrong when police started disappearing from the periphery of the protest. There's nothing a cop loves more than the chance to kick in some hippie teeth, so it had to be something big. One after the other I watched cops climb into their cruisers and speed off north through the town. I clambered into my beat-up old Chevy and tried to follow. Although I quickly lost sight of them, the growing confluence of sirens in the northern outskirts was hard to miss.

By the time I arrived, what had been a two-story home at the northern edge of the sprawl was little more than blackened walls surrounding a billowing bonfire. I slipped into a group of neighbors just outside the police's cordoned area. Firefighters desperately struggled to contain the blaze, which had begun devouring the walls of the neighboring homes.

"They're saying it was a gas explosion," said a housewife from a nearby home who had been out walking her dog. "Those poor kids…"

The story of the gas explosion in the home stuck around long after, though both myself and the police immediately knew better. There were four dead, Lucy among them, and nobody wanted to be the first ones to cast aspersions. A police source fed me an anonymous tip about nails embedded in the deceased, and I in turn urged them to put out a press release on it. Briefly, I wondered if someone else was to blame, someone who had slipped away north. But then I remembered the contents of Lucy's bag, and the anger she wore when she took it back.

Almost a year later the investigation was "sufficiently concluded" for the investigation to become public record. I wondered if that might have been the time to tell the whole story of the Druids. Surely I owed her that, at least. But I sat at the typewriter for an hour, unable to wring words from my heart. In the end, it didn't even matter. The deaths of the Druids were just another 70's bombing. A tragedy washed away by news of the Greenwich Village townhouse explosion, which occurred that year.

Yet in some fucked up way, the Druids did manage to buy T.O.M. a stay of execution. The planned leveling of the park didn't happen that week after all. Maybe the deaths of the Druids had brought just enough attention to their cause that the developer didn't want them to be martyrs. More cynically, I think that without their main opposition, there was no need to pay for rushed development.

Yet not long after the report went public, the development plans quietly moved forward. I would have missed it if my office hadn't gotten an anonymous call—I suspect from Seattle—to head down to Barlow Park. By the time I arrived, the equipment was already set up. A chainsaw whined as an orange-clad worker pressed it into the body of the enormous oak.

Before the whirring blade touched bark, I felt a rush of vindication. The moments where I accepted what T.O.M. was to the Druids were few and far between. In those moments I was full of hatred. If he had been real, he was the one who had poisoned their minds. If he was really what they thought, he was something I could blame for what happened to Lucy. Would Lucy and her friends have gone so far if they knew he had a brother? Had T.O.M. lied to them to try and save his own life?

When the chainsaw started working through the trunk, though, all of that dissipated. It was just a tree. All of this for a tree.

At the edge of the site, crouched in a patch of grass, I saw a similarly clad worker hunched over and rocking back and forth. His hands held the edge of his helmet against his chest to try to steady his shaking, and his face was lowered but a choked sob got through every couple seconds.

"Hey, are you alright?" I asked and the man shook his head.

"I don't know—" he stammered. He looked up with tears running down his cheeks from dilated eyes. "I feel like… I feel like we're doing something really wrong."

Regrets

"I came back to the park a few times after that and found an acorn. I assume it was from that tree, and sent it to a research buddy over in San Francisco."

"At the Botanical Research Institute?" Olivia asked. It was the same organization that tried to analyze that carnivorous plant Animal Control Officer Carl Satrum mentioned a year ago. The plant that attacked that little girl.

"That sounds about right. He mentioned it was a rare specimen of oak, one he hadn't seen before. I was left thinking it might have been extinct, but my friend suspects another of its kind might have taken root somewhere in San Cicaro."

"Maybe if the Druids had this, it might have helped with their civic case. Maybe the Druids wouldn't have had to go to the extremes they did. Maybe Lucy…"

Olivia could see the guilt on Gil's features. The way his breathing grew a little shallow, the way his hand clenched. Empathetically, she reached over and took his hand, giving it a light squeeze. Gil elicited no reaction, off in another time. Then he blinked and realized when he was. He shook his head and smiled, withdrawing his hand.

"Maybe I'm confused. Perhaps dementia."

Olivia laughed. "I don't know. Sounded pretty detailed if you ask me."

Gil waved for the check from the waiter. Olivia reached for her purse but Gil held out his hand to stop her.

"My treat. You pay for the next reminiscence."

"Fair enough," Olivia said. But she knew he was holding back something. Some detail or another that never made it beyond the first draft. Part of her wanted to know what really happened. If there was more to this than a "rare species of oak" that several people died trying to protect. But that was not a question she would dare risk.

Waving goodbye, she headed back towards the bus stop.

It was only a block away. Mercifully, no one occupied the bench, which looked clean aside from a little dust or pollen. Brushing it, she took a seat and leaned back, thinking over the day.

More than anything, she wanted to feel decent and hopeful again. America's prior decades sometimes felt like the Dark Ages, and she wanted, *needed*, to believe tomorrow would be better. Brighter.

Then she remembered. Stanley Gray, the philanthropist. The man who had helped found the Aquatic and Research Center. Taking out her phone, she brought up his Wikipedia article and began to peruse. Most of Gray's business partners did not have articles of their own, like Rosemary Lavoie or the strangely named "Mr. Plouton," with no given name.

But one man had a small article of his own. As Olivia read, she realized that although Stanley Gray got much of the credit, the work was done by another. An immigrant from Venezuela who made the city his home.

"Who are you," Olivia asked herself, "Mr. Mauricio Zambrano?"

Gold in the West

Ian Ableson

Mauricio's thoughts wandered as he watched the waves lap placidly at the beach. From the safety of his office the ocean looked so innocent, so alluring. Until one's gaze slid over to the warning signs that littered the beach, now professionally constructed of plastic and metal and covered in eye-catching graphics. Yet still bearing the same simple message after so many years.

DO NOT SWIM

While most of his memories of that time had blurred with the passing of the decades, he still remembered that day with crystal clarity. Even the face of Glenn Reed was little more than a suggestion in his mind nowadays, but he could picture the orange pearls scattered on the seabed as if he'd seen them yesterday.

Of course, the guilt of his partner's death had always lingered, an emotional scar that never faded. He wondered what Glenn would have to say about the San Cicaro Aquarium and Research Center. He wondered what Glenn would have to say about Mauricio himself, now almost ninety, founding member and director of such a respectable institution.

He imagined his old partner would find the whole notion very amusing.

"Hello? Excuse me? Are we doing this interview?"

The young woman's words snapped Mauricio from his reverie. He tore his gaze away from the window and focused on the applicant in front of him.

"My apologies, Miss Rachel. I was lost in memory. When you've lived as long as I have, you've collected a lot of them to sift through." He picked up her resume with his hands—they shook a little these days, but still had strength left in them—and peered at it through a pair of wire frame glasses. "So. You're applying for the position on the aquatic mammals team, yes? Want to work with the sea lions, hmm?"

"The large creatures were always my favorites, ever since I've been young. Not to mention I should probably do something with nearly a decade's worth of swimming practices."

"Strong swimmer then?"

"Well they *did* call me the shark."

"So I should hire a shark to handle the sea lions?"

"Absolutely," she quipped.

Good, Mauricio thought as he laughed. *One needs a certain amount of viciousness to survive in San Cicaro.*

"Well, your resume is quite impressive for your age. We'll move on to the technical section of the interview in a moment, but first I'd like to ask if you have any questions about the position."

"Yeah, I do. How big is the team, exactly? I mean, I don't mean any offense, but isn't it a little unusual for the Director of the whole aquarium to interview for an entry-level position?"

Mauricio hid a smile. Yes, she would do. Not a local, but she possessed the necessary resilience to do well in San Cicaro.

"It's very unusual," he said in agreement. "But I have been a part of this aquarium since before the building even existed, and as such I take immense personal pride in this institution. And besides, my colleagues and my wife have convinced me that it's finally time for me to retire. This position is the last one that will be hired while the institution is under my direction. It would be a shame for me to miss out on the interview."

She said nothing, but he could tell the girl's suspicions had been quelled. He glanced at her resume again. "So. Tell me about your internship with the Student Conservation Association…"

As the sun set over the horizon, Mauricio tied up his last few loose ends. He signed the offer letter for Rachel and dropped it off on the HR desk. He said his final goodbyes to the few straggling souls left in the building, and packed his briefcase. Before Mauricio departed his office at the San Cicaro Aquarium and Research Center, he took one final look out his window at ocean. To the fading gold in the west, to a sunset Mauricio wished Glenn Reed could have watched during his last moments.

"Our great plan never came to pass," Mauricio whispered with a bitter smile. "But if it wasn't for it… if it wasn't for you, we'd never have made this much of a difference. So long, partner."

Witness

A cold gust shocked Olivia, interrupting her reading, forcing her to rub her arms. It was late enough in September that an occasional cool night was nothing alarming. But this was more like the chill of the mountains.

Putting her hands in her pockets to warm her fingers, she felt a peculiar shape, and withdrew the Mahjong tile gifted to her by Xiomara. Sighing, she wondered why she had held onto the worthless trinket.

Until she flipped it over.

The plumb flower was there, but it had changed. Lines of blue, shaped like ice or snow, had lined the petals and vines. Details that did not exist before.

"What the hell…" she said. Maybe she had forgotten them? No, she was sure those symbols hadn't been there when it was first given to her. She made a note to ask someone knowledgeable about the game. Perhaps it was a gambler's trick piece, a fake that changed symbols using heat. Like a mood ring.

Olivia moved to put the tile back in her pocket when she noticed something in her peripheral vision. She turned her head to the left.

And gasped.

A shadowy figure stood in the night air, lanky in what might have been robes or a long coat. Where the street lights should have illuminated him, an obstinate darkness left him midnight clad. Faintly ethereal, an anthropomorphic thing of the void.

All save for those star bright eyes.

The cold no longer came from the air. It was *in* Olivia now. She stood, her skin puckering into gooseflesh, but she never took her eyes from the being. Her fight or flight instincts had abandoned her. She was frozen.

Perhaps she would have stayed like that forever, locked in a staring contest with the creature across from her, if what she had learned that day didn't rise to the forefront of her mind.

It took no small amount of will to force the words from her quivering lips. "You're… you're a Watcher…"

Only a brief dip of its eyes suggested a nod.

Olivia swallowed against her parched throat, racking her brain for anything she could ask. She no longer feared for her life or safety, but worried that any errant word or movement might send the Watcher away. "I… I met someone today who told me your people were… crowded out of San Cicaro."

He did not move.

"Others have kept your people from appearing too. And I know you're not really evil. You just are. Not good, not bad. You just watch, until people force your involvement."

He nodded again.

They're real they're real they're really real… A wellspring of excitement blossomed in Olivia's chest. Yet as the thoughts formed, a disturbing theory did as well. If the Dark Watchers existed, what else did? Ghostly sirens? Fairies who ate shadows? Witches?

Like the deep breath before the barbaric yawp… Xiomara's words echoed in Olivia's psyche. The question formed in her mouth like raindrops gathering in a puddle. "Is… is something going to happen? To this city? Like the Bath House?"

The starry eyes dipped lower than ever, nodding deeply.

"Will we be safe?"

The Watcher did not move for a while. Then, it raised a fuzzy hand. Olivia seized up, thinking it was about to point at her and *do* something. The fear returned abruptly.

The Watcher showed its palm.

And simply waved.

"Wait!" Olivia cried out. "Wait!"

The figure vanished, its body taken by the night as the twinkling twin lights of its eyes faded into the shadows.

Olivia could only watch the Watcher go. How could she begin to pursue something like that? As it departed, the air grew warmer again, a strange coincidence.

Why though? she thought. In all her reading from Dr. Walther Montgomery, never once were the Dark Watchers said to bring the winter with them. But that line stuck out to her again. *The heralds of a new era…*

Had she just imagined that? This was like no visual hallucination she'd read about. Panic gripped her. Maybe she was going mad? She looked around. Had anyone else seen it?

Her phone began to buzz from a notification, but she ignored it, still looking to where the Watcher had been, desperate to figure out exactly what she'd seen. It buzzed again. And again. And again.

Finally, she gave the obnoxious device a glance, and her eyes went wide. They were media updates, breaking news headlines. Warnings and alerts.

Local couple attacked by large animal in the historic district. Nearby residents urged to stay inside.

Rescue services dispatched to aid woman singing near Gatsby Rock.

BREAKING: Dozens of human bones discovered at San Cicaro Zoo.

> **Mom:** Olivia, are you okay?
> I heard a bus tipped over.
> You weren't on it were you

10 o'clock fire on Industrial Boulevard.

ALERT: Police in pursuit of man armed with sword near San Cicaro's Historic District.

> **Melissa:** I don't know
> what's going on but shit
> has hit the fan. Call Marco
> ASAP.

On and on it went.

It wasn't just her. It was everywhere.

Olivia turned off the notifications, lest her phone's battery die in the throes of its seizure-like updates. Not five minutes went by without another update, without another dangerous situation or bizarre incident. Problems the SCPD nor the city's residents could ignore.

Her head was pounding, the blood roaring through her ears. She dropped onto a bench before she fell down. Olivia gripped her phone with white knuckles as she read and waited. Watching as terror and panic began to replace everything she knew, block by block. There had always been whispers, rumors and hearsay. But it had never been like this. Never as insane as this.

San Cicaro had gone mad.

About the Authors

Adrianna Valencia is an artist and short horror fiction writer based in Northern California. She draws inspiration from local folklore and classic films, adding a dash of gothic horror to her stories. Her work has also been featured in The Other Stories podcast.

L.M. Charbonneau is a historian and human rights investigator. She lives and works in Edmonton, Alberta, Canada, where she can often be found running the river valley trails.

Alex Singer lives on coastal Connecticut with her wife, two cats, and too many sci-fi novels to count. Her short stories have appeared in Crossed Genres Magazine, Utopia Science Fiction, and Apparition Literature. For more, visit her website at littlefoolery.com or on Twitter @sfeertheorist.

Ian Ableson is an ecologist by training and a writer by choice. When not writing or hanging out with his wife and cats, he can often be found traversing wild places, clipboard in hand, collecting data on erratic birds and carnivorous plants.

Ichabod Ebenezer is the genre-promiscuous author of "A Shadow Stained in Blood" as well as countless short stories ranging from Horror to Sci-fi, from Fantasy to Mystery. He lives and writes in the Pacific Northwest with his family, a chameleon, and the ghosts of three cats. https://theichabodebenezer.com

J. Rohr is a Chicago native with a taste for history and wandering the city at odd hours. He currently writes articles for Horror Obsessive, 25YL Media, and his blog Honesty is Not Contagious as well as makes music in Beerfinger.

Vernon Miles lives in Washington D.C. and is a reporter with local news site ARLnow. When he's not working, he's hanging out with his rabbit George, building *Warhammer* figures or raiding with his *Destiny 2* clan.

Finally, the editors would like to thank Larry Kay for providing guest character Xiomara Chivara, previously depicted in *Welcome to San Cicaro*.

No city in the world has more strange sightings and unexplained mysteries per capita than San Cicaro. So when cub reporter Olivia Murphy strolls into her first official interview, even she knows better than to jump at every wild rumor.

Yet her unlikely source opens a Pandora's box of leads, many of which tie into a greater mystery involving the flora and fauna. For while humans may lie for fear of being labeled insane, Mother Nature plays no such games.

***Beasts of San Cicaro*. Available now on Amazon and SmashWords!**

In the troubled city of Strand, Governor's Guardsman Eirik struggles to fend off the criminal empires who rule the streets. But everything changes with the arrival of a powerful relic that belongs to the northern giants, threatening the security of the city itself. The thrilling prequel to Stoic's award-nominated *Banner Saga* trilogy!

***Banner Saga: The Gift of Hadrborg,* from Stoic. Available now on Amazon and SmashWords!**

Made in United States
North Haven, CT
22 February 2022